THE ONLY OUTCAST

THE ONLY OUTCAST

Julie Johnston

Tundra Books

Published in Canada by Tundra Books, *McClelland & Stewart Young Readers*,
481 University Avenue, Toronto, Ontario M5G 2E9

Published in the United States by Tundra Books of Northern New York,
P.O. Box 1030, Plattsburgh, New York 12901

Library of Congress Catalog Number: 98-60523

Canadian Cataloguing in Publication Data

Johnston, Julie, 1941–
     The only outcast

ISBN 0-88776-441-X (bound)   ISBN 0-88776-488-6 (pbk.)

I. Title.

PS8569.O387O54 1998   jC813'.54   C98-930887-1
PZ7.J66On 1998

We acknowledge the support of the Canada Council for the Arts for
our publishing program.

We acknowledge the financial support of the Government of Canada
through the Book Publishing Industry Development Program for our
publishing activities. Canadä

Design by Sari Ginsberg

Printed and bound in Canada

1 2 3 4 5 6   04 03 02 01 00 99

This book is dedicated to the memory of Larry Turner

J.J.

Acknowledgments

I am indebted to Kathy Lowinger for her enthusiasm, encouragement, and diligent editing, and to Sue Tate, who copyedited the manuscript. Thanks also for advice, research assistance, and the occasional turn of phrase to: Jane Collins, Lea Harper, Troon Harrison, Patricia Stone, Betsy Struthers, Florence Treadwell, Christl Verduyn, Julia Bell, Margaret Buffam, Suzanne Buffam, Andrea Green, Basil Johnston, Frank Johnston, Melissa Johnston, Kathleen Jordan, Diane Matheson, Leslie McMunn, Judith Preston, Ross Preston, Carl Rubino, Geraldine Rubino, Mary Ann Scott, Heward Stikeman, Lauren Johnston Stiroh, Leslie Johnston Tralli, Michael Treadwell, and Ann Wainwright; and to Susan Code, whose book, *A Matter of Honour* (General Store Publishing, 1996), contains stories based on Ottawa Valley folk history. "The Ferryman's Welcome" helped inspire Grandpa Hicks's tall tale.

I am grateful to Frances Turner and Don Canning for permitting me to make use of Larry Turner's book, *A Boy's Cottage Diary 1904*.

Contents

Foreword

The Only Outcast is based on the actual diary of sixteen-year-old Fred Dickinson written while at his relatives' cottage from July 27th – August 26th, 1904. It appeared in print in *A Boy's Cottage Diary 1904* (Petherwin Heritage, 1996), a history of early cottage life on Rideau Lake, compiled and written by Larry Turner.

The diary excerpts in this novel are partly invention and partly Fred's own words.

I

The Seventh Wonder
of the World of Freaks

Even inanimate objects have words.

The train pounded along steel rails: out-to-the-lake, out-to-the-lake, out-to-the-lake. We lurched around a curve and I swayed to the right, crowding my little sister, Bessie. She gave me a dark look as her hair bows danced against the window. I pulled out my new watch attached to a chain and checked the time: about seven minutes later than it had been last time I looked. The watch was a present from my father a week before my birthday. I closed it and ran my thumb across the engraving on the back, TO FREDERICK ON HIS 16TH BIRTHDAY, 2 AUGUST, 1904. Around its circumference were the words, TIME DISCOVERS TRUTH. You have to rotate it to read that.

"How long till we're there, Freddie?" Bessie asked.

"One thousand, eight-eight-eight hundred . . ."

She made a face like somebody falling over dead. "Seconds," I added.

She grabbed at my watch, but I yanked it back. She's only eight; seconds are still a mystery to her. She shriveled up her eyes and looked down her nose at me, reducing me to the size of something she could step on if she wanted to. Oh, she's got the haughty spirit down to a tee, all right. One day, I fully expect she'll marry some unsuspecting future emperor and start a war somewhere.

We were a good two-thirds of the way from Kemptville, where we live, to Perth, where our grandparents live. From Perth, Grandpa's boat would take us along the Tay Canal out to Rideau Lake. On the curve, the train lost a beat and changed its tune to Sunnybank-Sunnybank-Sunnybank: the name of Grandpa Hicks's summer cottage, our final destination.

Facing Bessie and me sat our brothers: young Tom, forehead pressed to the window; and Ernie, asleep, collar and tie hanging loose, chin bobbing on his chest. Bessie slumped down in her seat and stretched out her foot to kick Ernie awake. Without opening his eyes, he lifted his big boot and let it hover over the skirt of her pinafore, her Sunday best. (Ernie is two years younger than I am.) Bessie let out a roar and shrank toward the window, tucking in her dress on all sides.

Tom opened his window as far as it would go. "Will you look at that!" We were going over the railway bridge at Smiths Falls. Below we could see the Rideau Canal and a lock station. Clouds of steam from an excursion boat being locked through drifted up to mingle with steam from our locomotive. Passengers on the boat deck, some with parasols, waved at the train. Bessie waved back, and so did Tom until he looked back at Ernie and me with our arms folded across our manly chests. Tom is only ten. If someone granted Tom three wishes, they would be: to go everywhere Ernie and I go, to hear everything Ernie and I say, and to do everything Ernie and I do.

"Will you boys close that window? The soot's just pouring in. Really and truly!" It was the lady sitting behind Tom and Ernie. Tom banged the window shut, and the woman jumped and gasped as if he'd fired a cannon. She stood up and glared over the seat back at me, black specks all over her face, which she was smearing into streaks with her hanky. "Are you in charge of these hooligans?" she fumed.

"Ah-ah-ah-ah . . ." I could feel my face getting red and twisting out of shape in my effort to answer her. Bessie came to my rescue. "Yes," she said, "but it's not his fault. We behave like little salvages half the time, Papa says."

The woman frowned, more mystified, I think, than annoyed, and plumped back into her seat. I flashed ten fingers twice at Bessie to tell her it would be probably twenty minutes before we'd reach the town of Perth, but she didn't get it until I mouthed the word "twenty," and then she groaned and threw herself against the seat back to stare dully through the window. We both watched the procession of cedars, pines, and maples spin past and disappear down the long length of narrowing track behind us.

We've been making this trip every summer for the past five, alone for the past three since our mother died, so you might think we'd be used to it. The journey, I mean. We don't talk much about our mother, but that doesn't mean we're used to not having her.

Words are the bane of my life. With Ernie and Tom and Bessie, talk comes more or less easily. However, throw anyone else at me, or something that really needs to be said, and I go to pieces. I never know whether the words will come exploding out like gunshot, or disappear forever.

It drives Papa to his wit's end. He's trying to train it out of me so I'll be fit to go out and face the world like a man. We all had to go down to the station early today so that I could be the one to ask for the tickets. I practised in my mind, *Four tickets to Perth, please, four tickets to Perth, please*, and it came out just right. I handed over the money Papa had given me while he stood off to the side observing the way I handled myself. "Say," the ticket agent said to me, "how old are these two young ones?"

I glanced down at Tom and Bessie and felt the words flying apart inside my head, "T-t-ten and-and-and-and . . ."

"Eight," Bessie supplied.

I stole a look at my father, who stood with clamped lips staring at the sky asking God, I expect, why he'd been blessed with a tongue-tied dolt, instead of a son he could point to with pride. I saw Ernie shove his hands into his pockets and become deeply absorbed in the train schedule posted on the

4

wall. As for Tom, he stood where he was, looking from me to Papa and back to me as if he were the lord chief justice. "They go half fare," the ticket agent was saying, but I scarcely heard him. He put some change on the counter, which, in my embarrassment, I didn't notice. I walked away.

Slowly, enunciating every syllable, my father said, "Frederick, you forgot your change." Bessie handed it to me, and I passed it over to Papa, who stood there shaking his head. I lowered mine like a dog in disgrace.

Papa gave the agent a long-suffering shake of the head, and herded us outside into the brilliant sunshine. "Come! Come-come-come!" he repeated, holding the door open. Outside, as if I were deaf or not overly bright, he said loudly, "Frederick, you are nearly sixteen years old. When do you think you might begin to make even the slightest attempt to behave in a grown-up fashion?" I looked down at my boots, all scuffed and dusty, even though I'd polished them the day before. "Look at me when I'm speaking to you, Frederick."

When he talks like that I feel as if I've been sprinkled with hot pepper; my skin pricks and smarts and a splotchy rash comes out on my arms and neck and stomach, and I'd like to scratch but I don't because he hates to see people scratching in public. I wrenched my head up, knowing that my eyes were showing too much white, and that my neck was all red and skinny with a big bump where my Adam's apple wobbled because I was trying so hard to swallow.

He said, "Do you know, I think young Bessie here has more

strength of character, though she's just a girl, than you've ever thought of having." He paused to let the significance of this spread all over me. He sighed, and his voice sounded calmer. "What's wrong with you, son? It's weak to allow your nerves to get the better of you the way you do."

I nodded because it was easier than disagreeing. He's had to do a lot of altering and shifting of his dreams for me over the years. As a baby, I guess I showed a lot of promise that I didn't quite live up to. "I don't think our Fred will ever be the prime minister of Canada," I once heard him tell someone. He chuckled as if he'd said something funny, but I'm not so sure he found it all that humorous. I think he started off thinking I would become something he wasn't: a lawyer, maybe, or a teacher. Eventually his dream dwindled down to one last faint hope: that I could settle in to work in his dry-goods store, learn the business, and take over when he gets old. But I guess even that's out of the question. He finds it too nerve-racking to have me stuttering and stumbling around him all day. "No, son," he says, "the best place for you is some kind of work in the city where you'll have to compete. Toughen you up." He's written to someone he knows in Toronto, hoping to get me started this summer – a trial run of sorts – but, so far, he's not had a reply.

Papa looked at his watch. "Well, make the most of your time, Frederick. Your mother used to put great store by living on the lake like a pack of savages. Perhaps she was right; I don't know. My only hope is, that you'll try to pull yourself together this summer. When you come back from the lake, I want to be able to say, 'Frederick, my boy, I'm proud of you.'" He gave me a pat on the back that felt more like a swat. It caught me off balance and I staggered forward, coming down hard on Bessie's foot. She didn't let out so much as a squeak. He's right. She's a very manly little girl.

The train appeared then, looming out of the distance, wailing, chuffing, bearing down on us. I stood close to the track until Tom started yanking on my arm, pulling me back. "I wish Papa wouldn't get so angry with you," he said over the sound of the train.

I looked back at Papa busy with Bessie's valise, out of earshot. "He's not-not-not really angry, just ex-ex-ex . . ." I wanted to say "exasperated," but the word broke into pieces and disappeared. We began to file aboard the train then, and Papa called after me, "If I get a reply about a job, I'll come and fetch you home." I nodded maturely before hotfooting it up the steps into the coach, tripping at the top. I'm not what you would call nimble.

Rattling along in the train, I undid the watch-chain's clasp attached to my trousers and dangled the watch in front of Bessie. She pounced on it. "Can I open it?"

"May I."

She curled the corner of her lip at me meaning, Don't bother me with details, and released the catch. The lid sprang open to reveal the elegant watch face. She studied it, squinting, lips pushed out. "It's almost XI to I," she said.

Tom leaned across to take a look. "It's five to one." He gave Ernie and me a superior grin.

"I was speaking Roman," Bessie said. "Which is a foreign language," she added grandly.

I held out my hand for the watch.

The train lost speed as we neared Perth, whistle shrieking, bell cling-clang-clanging. We hissed and wheezed to a stop beside the stone station with its flared overhang, squat as a toad under a toadstool. My mother's sister Auntie Ede, one of our unmarried aunts, was there to meet us, along with our cousin Harold, Auntie Lizzie's son. People often say to Grandma, "Oh, the Hickses are such a close-knit family." It's true, I guess. Auntie Ede, Auntie Min, and Uncle Will all live at home in Perth with Grandma and Grandpa. None of them got married. Auntie Lizzie, the eldest, is a widow and she lives just up the street with her two children, our cousins, Harold and Ettie. My mother was the second of the Hicks girls, as they're sometimes called, even now. We visit my father's side, the Dickinsons, too, but mostly we visit the Hickses.

From under the low-slung brim of his cap, cousin Harold was watching us get down from the train, standing back to let Auntie Ede grab each of us for the I'm-so-glad-to-see-you kiss. I managed to sidle past my brother Ernie, who was in her clutches and had a kind of toothache look about him, his face squinched to one side. I took this opportunity to bend over to tighten my bootlace, so Auntie Ede ended up patting me on the back. I don't know why women are forever trying to smack their lips against us fellows. I hope Bessie never takes it up. Perhaps I'll have a word with her.

I hadn't seen our cousin Harold since last Christmas. I noticed him give me the once-over, stacking up my height against his own. I dragged my watch out of my pocket, flicked it open, glared at the time, and snapped it shut. I yawned, bored with pocket watches and trains. And cousins. He looked about a head taller than me, but I think he had thick soles on his boots.

Grandma had a big spread laid out for us when we got to the house on North Street. Even before we opened the screen door, everything smelled like a combination of cinnamon and apples and bread just out of the oven. Through the open windows you could hear a saw buzz the dense heat of the afternoon from Grandpa's carriage works down the street. Grandma greeted us with another round of kisses. "Well, now, you just missed your Uncle Will. He's gone back to the shop early; they're that shorthanded with Grandpa at the lake all summer. Sit down, sit."

His jaws working over a hunk of fresh bread, cousin Harold said, "I've been having myself a swell time helping out in the shop. Uncle Will says I'm a natural."

A natural pain in the anatomy, I was thinking, but I said, "I-I-I might have a job, one-one-one of these days."

"Doing what? Cleaning outhouses?" He thought this was a real thigh slapper, and he even got Ernie laughing when he pretended to shovel and hold his nose at the same time. When he finally calmed down he said, "Relax. Nobody's going to hire a runt. You're not strong enough yet, laddie, nor old enough." He's all of six months older than me, yet he has this snide way of grinning at me as though he's just caught me sucking my thumb.

I guess I had put my fork down and was scowling into my potato salad because Grandma started in at me. "Eat, lad, eat. You'll never grow into a big strong man at this rate."

"I know."

"And there's pie for dessert, two kinds."

"I know."

She shook her head at Auntie Ede. "I don't know who he takes after. Nobody in this family, certainly." She was right. Where the others were fair, I was dark. Ernie, Tom, and Bessie wore sunny smiles most days. People said I looked weighed down. The Hickses were plump; I was a scarecrow.

"Oh, he's like Ida was," Auntie Ede said. "You know that." Ida was my mother. "Don't you remember how slight she was at that age, Mother? Rail thin the summer she turned sixteen."

Grandma took my chin and turned my face sideways, nodding. "His face is his own, though, isn't it? But you're right; she was awful thin at that age." She gave me back my chin and I thought I saw a little bit of moisture just behind her eyes, which made my own prickle. Quietly, she said, "As a wee one, though, wasn't he just the dead spit?" I cut a slice of ham into five pieces, speared them all, and forked them into my mouth.

"Why aren't I the dead spit of Mummy?" Bessie said. "I'm the girl."

I escaped after our meal into the cool and shadowy parlor while the ladies did the dishes, not so much assisted as entertained by Bessie, who recognized a captive audience when she saw one. Ernie was there ahead of me. Harold had gone up the street to his house to pack his gear for our trip to the lake, and to make rope handles for the tent we would have to carry to the family boathouse on the canal at the edge of town. The sleeping quarters at the cottage were already filled to capacity with adults – Grandpa, Auntie Lizzie (Harold's mum), Auntie Min (the youngest of the Hicks girls), Harold's older sister Ettie, Uncle Will (who sometimes goes out after work and on weekends), and Grandma and Auntie Ede when they choose to go out, leaving only enough room for Tom and Bessie. This year, Grandpa decided we older boys had better camp in a tent.

I stood in the parlor doorway of the Perth house, gazing around as I always do. Ernie was looking through the stereoscope at views of Niagara Falls – said to be one of the seven natural wonders of the world and probably the only one I'll ever get to see.

Above the fireplace hangs a picture of Grandpa in his younger days: an explosion of hair and whiskers jutting from his head like a lion's mane. He looks like someone in the Bible, one of those fellows who begat everybody else. He loves the lake and says he'd holiday there year-round if it wasn't for his blasted "arthur-itis."

Grandma has her own views. She says, "You can't tell me it's a holiday when I have to haul water from the lake to wash clothes, wash dishes, wash myself, and, on top of that, cook for twice as many people in a kitchen that's half the size of the one in town, using that cookstove we took to the lake because it was too temperamental to use in town. You can rough it in the wilderness if you like," she tells him. "I, for one, like my creature comforts and that's that."

I can't imagine spending the summer anywhere other than Sunnybank – the name Grandpa gave the cottage and the curve of shore it sits on. If you want to see boats, that's the place to be as it's just a five-minute walk from the locks. We see almost every boat on the lake – the ones going to or from Perth, at any rate. The major ones are the *Jopl* and the *Westport*, both steam-powered freight boats, and the *Aileen*, a small steamer running cruises and delivering passengers and mail. If we look through Grandpa's field glass, we get a good view of the boats in the channel as they travel between Ottawa and Kingston. Our favorites are the large excursion steamers, the *Rideau King* and the *Rideau Queen*. And as for fishing, swimming, or lazing in a hammock under a tree with a good book, you can't beat Sunnybank. It's a fine location.

In the parlor, I had made my way to the upright piano at the end of the room. On it were some dried roses in a picture frame. They came from my mother's funeral and are twined with a lock of her hair. Beside that is my mother's photograph taken three years ago, a few months before she died. I stared into her face and tried to see myself in her broad forehead and wide-set eyes. She stared straight out at me as if she were about to open her mouth to tell me something. I tried to remember the sound of her voice and couldn't at first, and then after a moment, I could. *Frederick?* I heard, the sound going up at the end the way it did when she used to call me in from outside.

Ernie put the stereoscope back and stood looking over my shoulder. I said, "Can you remember wh-wh-what she looked like?"

He stepped back and looked at me as if I were crazy. "You're staring right at her."

"No, I mean what she really looked like, not in a-a-a picture."

"Pictures are all we've got."

I said, "They make everything s-s-so s-s-s-set, as though that's all there was of her, only this one-one-one pose."

Ernie didn't say anything. He turned around and walked out of the room. He hates when I talk about things like that. Too bad Ernie isn't the eldest, then I'd have someone to look up to. Nothing rattles him. He's like a human compass the way he knows how to steer clear of emotional booby traps.

The *Bessie* boat, Grandpa's pride and joy, purred along, cutting a wide swath through the flat brown water of the Tay Canal. On either side of the cut stood floating fields of bulrush and reeds, waving after us as they met our swells. Off to our right, the sun hung low like a fireball singeing the tops of the reeds. Red-winged blackbirds flitted and perched on sturdy cattails, and swallows dipped and arced in their search for mosquito snacks. A present to me from Grandma poked through the top of my carpetbag under the deck – a maroon leather book with blank pages. She gave it to me just before we pushed off from the boathouse. "It was your mother's," she said. "She used to keep diaries when she was about your age. This must have been a spare one we've had hanging around for years."

"Why didn't you give it to me?" Bessie pouted, "I'm the girl." I saw Harold give Ernie a nudge. He pitched his voice way up high. "Dear Diary," he said, "I was so provoked at Bessie today. Someday I'll give her such a smack! Bye-bye for now. Fondly, Fred." Ernie and Tom laughed their beans off.

From the wharf Grandma called, "Now, that'll do," and Auntie Ede said, "Don't be always at Freddie, you lads. He has problems enough without your teasing and making him feel odd man out." I don't know what she and Grandma think of me, or what any of them think, for that matter. That I'm the seventh wonder of the world of freaks, possibly, and can't stand up for myself.

Uncle Will is captain of the *Bessie* boat this summer, now that Grandpa's arthritis is so bad. He didn't feel it necessary to add his two cents' worth, which I appreciated. He got the engine going smartly and, with the smell of gasoline fumes in our noses, we waved good-bye to those on shore, mighty glad to be finally underway on the last lap of our journey to Sunnybank. Other people had gathered to admire the Hicks family's boat. It's gasoline-powered, one of the first on Rideau Lake. The *Bessie* (named after guess who) is long and sleek, and cuts through water like a hot knife through butter. It is capable of speeds of up to eight miles an hour.

I was wondering what I would write in the book. Not sissy stuff like Harold was ranting about. Harold's not a bad egg once you get used to him, but he has to torment a fellow just to get his digs in. I was getting kind of excited about those tempting, blank pages. I might write about this boat in it: gleaming oak on the inside, white on the outside with red and blue trim. I'm going to ask Uncle Will to teach me to operate it when he's not too busy. I could put in our adventures at the lake: Harold with a fatal dose of poison ivy, Bessie getting kidnapped by slave traders, except they'd bring her back. More trouble than she's worth. But, of course, nothing like that ever happens at the lake. Each day rolls into the next. Sunny, cloudy, rainy sometimes, and we boys larking around having a fine time, and that's about it. I expect that's what I'll end up writing about.

I've been thinking, maybe a diary is like a photographer's picture. You don't get to see all the stuff that happens before a picture's taken, or after it, either. In a diary, it's about the same. If you want to know everything that goes on in the life of a diary writer, I imagine you're out of luck, unless you can read between the lines.

Explorers keep journals. I had the opportunity to read some passages from Sir Henry Stanley's records this past May. They appeared after Stanley died, in the paper Papa gets. "How I Found Livingstone" was one, and "In Darkest Africa" was another. You find out a lot about the wilds of Africa and about the hardships of being an explorer, but you don't find out how scared he was, or whether he made any stupid blunders, or had any embarrassing moments. Because people are going to read it, that's why. In photographers' pictures you don't find out how people looked most days of the week because they're all dressed up and slicked down for the camera.

I will write: *Herein lies an account of my days at darkest Sunnybank.*

2

Reading Between the Lines

It is about 7 miles from Perth to the lake along the Tay Canal, and we got down it in about 50 minutes. If we had hitched up Nellie to Grandma and Grandpa's buggy and gone by the road, it would have taken longer. We did not lock through as Uncle Will had to go back again later that evening. Auntie Lizzie (Harold's mum) and Auntie Min and cousin Ettie met us at the upper locks, and we all walked down to the cottage carrying the tent and the baggage. Grandpa, unable to walk to the locks for his arthritis, was very glad to see us.

We're calling our campground Beaver Camp at Grandpa's suggestion. He thought we should pitch the tent in a clearing behind the cottage so we wouldn't have too far to walk to the outhouse. (He believes the whole population suffers from arthritis.) We chose, instead, a place downhill from the cottage – a flat point of land jutting out into the bay. It's sheltered by a few trees and has an ideal spot for a campfire complete with logs to sit on. For camouflage we have a large field of daisies waltzing in the breeze between our tent and the cottage, making it difficult for the cottage folk to keep an eye on us, although we can spy on them quite handily when we want to.

It was late before we got to putting the tent up and, just before we did, I lay on my back for a moment or two in the clearing we'd made and gazed up at what looked like spilled ink seeping through an orange sky. Its dampness touched my face. Dew, probably. Around the edge of my vision, silvery birch leaves dangled like wind chimes.

"Lazy bum! On your feet!" That was Ernie calling me back to reality. We got the tent up with a minimum of bickering, and it looked fairly roomy with a swell bed we made by putting an oilcloth and blankets over a pile of hay. Tom's been clamoring to be let sleep with us, but there isn't enough room for four. Bessie says she wouldn't sleep anywhere near a pack of smelly boys even if you paid her.

It's after ten o'clock now, and the moon is up along with a sky full of stars. Auntie Lizzie has lent us a small trunk for our coats and good trousers so the mice won't make nests in them. This will become our table if we want to eat inside. Our formerly spacious tent is now packed to the hilt with a crate of cooking pots and dishes and another of provisions. We scavenged a piece of driftwood from the shore, which we've propped up inside for our clothes to hang on. There's no floor in the tent so we have quite a few ants and spiders sharing our location. We've dug a drainage ditch around us in hope of keeping out rainwater.

Our bed looks big, but when you get three boys in it, it automatically shrinks. "My God, Harold, don't you ever trim your toenails?" Ernie said. I could have said the same to him when he rolled over and scraped right through to bone on my ankle. I was doing a lot of squirming trying to get comfortable, which Ernie, in the middle, didn't appreciate. He said, "I'd prefer it if you didn't use my eye as your elbow rest."

We could no longer hear any sounds from the cottage folk, who seemed to have settled in for the night. The frogs were holding a concert in the long grass outside our tent, and we could hear the loons calling out to each other across the water. One seemed to call, "Are you there? Are you there? Are you there?" And from a distance her mate answered, "Won't be l-o-o-o-ng. Back so-o-o-on."

Ernie sat up, taking the covers with him. "What's that?"

"Just the loons."

"No, listen!"

The high-pitched whine of a mosquito buzzed my head and then another and another. Hundreds of them. Droves. We ducked our heads under the covers for protection. "I'm getting smothered," Ernie gasped. "It stinks down here."

Harold threw off the covers. "I'm gettin' the heck out of this place!" He untied the tent door and scrambled out while Ernie and I yelled at him for letting in more mosquitoes. We could see him outside waving his arms like a madman. Pretty soon I went out, too, and began pulling up the long green grass that grew beside the water. Ernie thought I'd gone mad, and stood there swatting at his neck and his arms until he figured out what I was doing, and pitched in to help. Harold was still running back and forth in his shirttail, working up a sweat, attracting more mosquitoes. I got some hay from our bed, and made a little pile of the whole mess of grass and hay on the ground near the foot of our bed. "Where are the matches?" I asked Ernie.

"Harold put them someplace."

"Come and help us find-find-find the matches, Harold," I yelled and, after a minute, he came into the tent to see what we were up to.

"Matches?"

"We-we-we need a smudge fire to keep the mosquitoes away."

Harold rummaged around in the dark, knocking over our pile of dishes and scattering our food supplies, trying to locate the matches. He finally found them where he'd left them for safekeeping and easy access – in his left boot. I struck the match on the hard earth and put it under the grass and hay until it smoldered, sending up a plume of smoke, and we got back into bed.

Ernie coughed. "Pretty smoky, isn't it?"

"Well, sure it's s-s-s-smoky. How else are we going to fight-fight-fight off the skeeters?"

Harold began to cough. "It's killing me," he croaked.

"A little bit of smoke isn't going to hurt you," I tried to say, but I was coughing so hard I couldn't get my breath. All three of us made a lunge for the door. Outside we bent over, coughing our insides up and spitting on the ground. Smoke billowed out through the door flap of our tent, clouds of it.

"I hope you boys aren't taking up smoking." That was Auntie Lizzie's voice reaching us from the cottage veranda.

"We're smoking mosquitoes, Mother," Harold called back.

"It'll stunt your growth," she called in a warning voice.

We sat in our shirttails and bare feet under the moon, listening to the water slurp at the shore, watching smoke drift out of our tent. We could hear slap, swat, slap coming from the veranda. After the smudge died down, we went back inside our tent and fell asleep.

All you could see of the sun next morning when we staggered out of our smoky tent was a promising, peachy haze behind treetops on the other side of the lake. On our side, the moon was still hanging there, not especially shiny, surprised that morning had sneaked up on it. In the early half-light, it felt like I'd stumbled into a new land where time hadn't been worked out yet. It could have been night or it could have been day. I put my watch in the trunk, in the pocket of my Sunday trousers.

Ernie is very good at issuing orders. He had Harold chinning himself on the rafters in the boathouse looking for our fishing rods, and me stumbling around tripping over the sail in the half-light while he went after worms with a spade and a tin pail. "Got everything?" he asked when he came back with the bait.

"Oars," I said.

"There's a good stiff breeze," he said. "We don't need oars."

"B-b-b-better take a paddle, at least."

"Yes, Granny."

We were underway, finally, in the *Jumbo*, an oversized rowing skiff, with a place for a mast and sail. The breeze was brisk and, with the sail up, we scooted along ahead of it, racing the waves as far as the bass beds, our surefire bass-catching spot up the north shore from our camp. We took down the sail to drift along the edge of what we call the drowned lands – an area now covered by water from the time the Rideau Canal was built. If you look down into the shallows between lily pads large as plates, you see what looks like a horizontal forest of fallen trees. Black bass laze in the green murk here among leafless branches and scheme to outsmart us.

Seaweed (lakeweed, we should call it) scuffed the sides of

the *Jumbo*. "Throw out the anchor, Harold," Ernie said. Harold looked under the seat in the back of the boat, but it wasn't there.

"Good old Freddie forgot to put it in," he said. Ernie looked at me with a pained expression.

"Who needs it?" I said. "We're not-not-not drifting." But we were. The wind seemed to pick up strength as the sunrise spilled over the tops of trees, and soon we were drifting away from the bass beds and up the lake toward a sandy stretch, a place where we liked to swim. The fish were happy with our change of plans. We pulled the boat up onto the sand. There were no other boats on the lake and no cottages along this part of the shore. No one else would even want to be up this early in the morning. We stripped down for a splash fight in the waist-high water. All the while, we kept our eyes peeled for fishermen.

We soon got tired of mucking about in the shallows, with sandy clay squishing up over our feet as far as our ankles. It made us think of quicksand. We pushed the *Jumbo* out into deeper water, and soon were having ourselves a ripping time jumping off the bow of the boat, turning somersaults, and landing with a splat on our bare backsides in the water. Each time we did, we had to swim a little farther to catch up to the boat drifting with the wind up the lake. We were still a good half-mile below Rideau Ferry. This is a little hamlet that now has a swing bridge spanning the lake, but back in the old days you could only cross the lake by means of a ferry. There are stories about this ferry operation that would give you the jitters for the remainder of your life if you were gullible enough to believe them. Anyway, the name of the place is Rideau Ferry and not Rideau Swing Bridge.

It wasn't exactly a contest, but as we clung to the side of the boat to catch our breath, we were shrewdly watching each other perform before clambering onto the bow ourselves to do one better. I figured I could do a corking good swan dive if I could get enough height. I gave the bow a whopping bounce, which catapulted me high into the air. I spread my arms like wings and soared out over the water.

And – Lord-thundering-Almighty! A rowboat! In full view! It appeared like a nightmare out of nowhere. Just before the top of my skull hit the water, I had a vision of a beautiful girl with pink cheeks and wild dark hair sitting in the front of that boat with a fishing rod. I plunged deep, hoping with all my heart that it was some kind of mirage, because if it wasn't, how could I show my face up there?

I stayed underwater, turning this way and that, paddling my hands, looking up toward the surface for a glimpse of the bottom of the *Jumbo*. And then I saw it above me, a dark shadow in my algae-green underworld. If I came up on the far side of it, I could shield myself from the boat with the girl in it. My lungs were fit to burst as I propelled myself above the surface, grabbing the side of the boat with a gasp, shaking my wet hair out of my eyes.

She gave a small, polite scream.

"I say!" I heard the man – the other occupant of the boat – remark. He positioned his oars above the water, ready to clip me a good one if I tried to accost them further. I let go of their gunwale and swam like blazes for our boat, which Ernie and Harold had towed by the rope behind them back to the sandbar. They had somehow slithered into it and shamefaced, heads down, were huddled over bunched-up clothes in their laps, staring at the floorboards, trying to look invisible.

"Mortified" would be the word to use if I were going to enter this in my diary, which I'm not. From the corner of my eye, I watched the man in the other boat putting a lot of muscle into pulling the oars, and the man and girl were soon up the lake and out of sight. The girl hadn't even so much as turned around. My teeth were chattering hard enough to fall out of my head as I crouched in the shallow water on the far side of the *Jumbo*.

"Your lips are turning purple," Ernie observed once the other boat had gone, now that he no longer needed to be invisible. I gave us a push off the sandbar before climbing in, and we all wrestled ourselves into our clothes.

"Ho-o-o!" Ernie started to giggle. "Did you see the girl? Holy mackerel! The look on her face!"

Harold said, "She took one look at Fred swanning over the water in his birthday suit and just about dropped dead."

"She did-did-didn't!" I whispered. My voice wouldn't go any louder. "Did she?" I looked at Ernie for the truth.

"She wouldna dropped dead. I think she was laughing."

"She wasn't laughing," Harold said, "she was hy-sterical."

"I bet she could-could-couldn't really see me. They weren't that close."

"Any closer and they'd have hollered for the police. You coulda landed in her lap."

Ernie and Harold ran the sail up. It crackled as the wind whipped it, filling it, and we tacked across the lake like chain lightning. The rowboat with the girl in it would have been up near Rideau Ferry by now, probably going under the bridge. It wasn't a boat we'd ever seen on this part of the lake before. It wasn't a boat, I hoped, we'd ever see again.

We were in the widest part of the Lower Rideau. The wind was gusty, making it hard to steer a course. The *Jumbo* has no centerboard, just a long rudder, so it took nearly all my strength leaning on the tiller to bring us about. We tacked back across the lake and could see Beaver Camp now, our white tent dull against the gleaming birches on the rock-lined point. Behind it, well back from the shore in a grove of its own, Sunnybank rose like an oversized anthill above the long grass, smoke drifting above its chimney. You could just see the boathouse tucked into its own little cove between camp and cottage. The Union Jack was flying from the flagpole on the front dock, which meant Grandpa was up doing his chores, raising the flag being one of them. Auntie Lizzie would be boiling water for the porridge.

"We'd better take her in," Ernie called to me.

"We're too fast," I yelled.

"Bring her about then!"

"I can't!" I was leaning on the tiller as hard as I could. The wind had us and was playing us for fools. The sail whipped and billowed. "Take the-the-the." I was trying to say, "Take the sail down," but it wouldn't come out. I was making faces and pointing at the sail, and all Ernie could do was scream at me to steer the damn boat. I threw up my hands to tell him it was impossible and, with a look of disgust, he clambered back to the stern and grabbed the tiller, shoving me off the seat, upsetting the pail of worms. At the same moment the wind came gusting from all directions at once. It took the sail, whipping it 180° the wrong way.

We were shipping water badly. By now we were all screaming, telling each other what to do. "The boom's wedged!" Harold yelled. He tried to pull the sail down, but it was jammed. We washed along on a tilt, heading straight for the rocky point jutting out from shore. Harold yelled, "Holy Moses! We're gonna crash! We're gonna die!"

We were going to crash, all right. Grandpa's boat would be smashed to pieces. I sat on the floorboards where Ernie had pushed me. I knew we should get the sail down, but figured Ernie would have a better plan. I sat there waiting, just sat there expecting him to perform a miracle with the useless tiller. Harold was crouched in the bow with his arms over his head expecting death. We were within seconds of piling up on the rocks. The sail, full and billowing, still had a mind of its own.

Ernie was staring straight ahead with his mouth open, and what went through my head was, *He doesn't know what to do.* In that split second I thought, *He can't save us.* Then I saw Harold move toward the mast and, at almost the same moment, so did I. We tilted again and I lost my balance, slipping on the worms in the water sloshing about in the bottom of the boat. I think Harold thought I was trying to jump ship. He grabbed the mast, yanking up, pulling on it, trying to take it down. Ernie saw what he was doing, and between them they toppled the mast, bringing the sail down with it. It drooped into the water, slowing us down, and we drifted peacefully in to shore.

We were all breathless, and Harold was swearing in a relieved kind of way. I couldn't look at Ernie because I've always reckoned he could do anything better than anyone else on earth. "We were nearly goners," Harold said.

"The sun was in my eyes," Ernie said. "I could have brought us around if I hadn't been just about blinded."

"Mincemeat!" Harold said. "All over the rocks."

"The stupid wind!" Ernie said. "You can't tell which way it's blowing at this end of the lake."

They went on talking about the close call, embellishing it, altering it, making it something they could live with, and didn't say anything to me or even look at me. I had been only a passenger, it seemed, of no more importance to the operation than the squished, half-drowned worms.

Ernie said, "We're not telling anyone about this." Harold

agreed. "Grandpa would have our heads!" Almost in silence, we did some minor repairs on the rudder and the boom and took a sponge to the inside of the boat. We acted as though nothing had happened.

3

The Hoofprint of the Devil

We got up before the sun yesterday intending to fish, but instead went for a sail in the Jumbo. After we got back, we made an excellent stove out of stones and some iron sheeting we found near the locks. Harold and Ernie put on a ripping fire in the stove for the cook (me) to get breakfast. We had force, boiled eggs, syrup, very strong coffee, bread, etc. Grandpa invited us to spend the rest of the morning trimming trees in the grove, and collecting pine knots for kindling for the cottage stove in return for some pocket money.

Bessie, Harold's sister Ettie, and Auntie Min perched on a nearby log while we ate our breakfast. Ettie considers herself a grown-up now that she's nineteen and has young gentlemen coming to call. She spends a lot of time making neat coils of her braids, and then pulls wisps of hair out of them to make a halo round her face. It looks quite fetching, in a way. Auntie Min isn't much older than she is, but doesn't have a knack with hair. Hers is scraped back so tight it looks painful. Sometimes they're great chums, and sometimes they get on each other's nerves to the point where Auntie Lizzie casts dark looks at both her sister and her daughter and says, "Lord preserve us! Why wasn't I born a hermit?"

Tom joined us, standing over us with his hands in his pockets and his feet planted wide, as if he planned to take root in our presence. Whenever she looked at our piles of food, Bessie made little gagging sounds, which she changed to pig grunts when any of us forked more grub onto our plates.

"Where did you go, early this morning?" Ettie asked us.

"Yeah!" said Tom, looking as if he expected a pack of lies.

"Nowhere," I said.

"Fishing," Ernie said.

"Swimming," Harold said.

Bessie said, "They're fibbing."

"No we're not. We meant to go fishing," Ernie explained, "but we ended up swimming down near the bathing place until we saw . . ."

"We didn't see-see-see anything," I said loudly. "We just got cold and came home."

"Freddie's blushing," Bessie said. "You can always tell when that boy has a secret. He turns into a tomato."

"You might have included me," Tom said. He began scuffing the toe of his boot into the dirt in front of us, where we sat cross-legged on the ground, shoveling down our breakfast.

"Cut it out," I said when sand flew into my already muddy-looking coffee.

We could see Grandpa making his way toward us through the long grass, leaning heavily on a walking stick he'd carved from a sapling. "What's this, what's this?" he said. "Still eating breakfast and the morning half gone! Have we a bad case of slug-abed-itis on our hands?"

Auntie Min put in a good word for us. "They've been up since dawn gallivanting all over the lake, apparently."

"No fish to show for their troubles, I see," Grandpa said, peering into our dishes and pots. He lowered himself creakily onto a stump and leaned over his stick. "Understand there's to be an evening social up at Oliver's Ferry on the hotel lawn."

The place was called Oliver's Ferry before it was called Rideau Ferry, but only old folks call it that now. Or people who want to scare the gizzard out of you. Oliver was the villain who operated the ferryboat, way back about eighty years ago. You hear so many stories about him, it's hard to know what's true and what isn't.

Grandpa went on gabbing about the social. "There'll be all manner of sweets, they say, including ice cream."

"Can I go?" Tom asked, but no one answered.

"Smiths Falls band'll be there, too, I hear."

Tom kept saying, "Can I go, can I go?"

"You lads have any interest in earning some pocket money?"

We admitted that we did, so he kindly sentenced us to a morning of hard labor. We called Tom to join us, but he was reading the funny papers and couldn't put them down. "Later," he said, "after I read one more page." We took the rake and the saw and a hatchet and a wheelbarrow into the grove, and set to work gathering pinecones and sawing dead branches off the red and white pines that grow there so close you can scarcely see the light of day. Tom didn't appear, but we hadn't really expected he would.

The wind went down about noon and it rained for a little while, though hardly enough to wet us where we were working in the grove, but we quit anyway. We brought in our pine knots and kindling to the cottage folk, who took pity on us and cooked us some noonday dinner. "This'll put a damper on the social tonight, if it keeps up," Auntie Lizzie said after dinner. She filled the large dishpan with water from the kettle while Ettie, Auntie Min, and Bessie stood by with dish towels.

"Oh, I don't think so," Grandpa said. He was looking all over for his pipe and found it under the newspaper Uncle Will had brought him the night before, a brown hole singed into the back page. "That rain isn't going to . . . amount to a . . . hilla beans." He was lighting his pipe, taking long draws on it while giving his weather pronouncement. As pipe smoke filled the kitchen, the aunties and cousin Ettie started waving their hands around like fans and saying, "Whew, pew," until Grandpa took his pipe outside to the veranda.

He was right. By evening, after our camp supper consisting of a tin of pork and beans, fried potatoes, cookies, biscuits, and bread, the sky cleared. Uncle Will had come out from town in the *Bessie* boat and, after supper, asked "Who's for a boat ride?" At high volume, Tom and Bessie let him know that they were first in line. Then the ladies said they'd be pleased to go, and Grandpa said, if he ever managed to get himself in, he'd sure as shootin' never get himself out again, so he'd stay home and keep house.

When they all piled into the boat, Tom noticed that we older fellows were hanging back. "We've got more exciting things to do," Harold called as he untied the *Bessie* boat for them and shoved it off. You could see a look of outrage on Tom's face as he remembered the social. "Take me with you," he bellowed.

"Got any m-m-money?" I called from the shore.

"Treat me for once," he yelled. He had his arms out imploring us to yank him out of the *Bessie* boat, which was ten feet out from shore by now. Uncle Will waved, grinning at us, knowing he had solved our little-brother problem for us. He headed the *Bessie* down the lake toward the Poonamalie

Lock, and we got into the *Jumbo* with two sets of oars in place and headed up the lake to Rideau Ferry. The last we saw of Tom, he had his fingers hooked into the corners of his lips, making faces at us as the *Bessie* cut majestically through the calm water, her wake a regal train.

Rowing the *Jumbo*, it took us exactly thirty-seven minutes by my watch to get to Rideau Ferry. This settlement is really tiny. It grew into a place after the bridge was built, I guess. At either end of the bridge, there are a few houses built close to the road. On the Perth side, there's a very smart hotel, which attracts city folk. Fishermen from the United States like it, too. Beside it there's a store that doubles as a post office.

Other boats were tied at what we call the government dock, but we found a spot near one end. We could hear the Smiths Falls brass band playing "Drink to Me Only with Thine Eyes." The sight of crowds of people milling about on the hotel lawn nearly made me stay behind on the dock, but I decided I wouldn't have to talk much to any of them, and caught up to Harold and Ernie, who were heading straight for the ice cream table.

I stood there watching a boy turn the crank on the ice cream bucket, wondering if he got to eat as much as he wanted, and how you would go about getting a job like that. "What kind can I get you, young man, strawberry or vanilla?" the woman behind the table asked me.

"S-s-s-s . . ." I began, but realized I'd never get it out. "'Nilla," I heard myself shout.

35

"I'm not deaf," the woman said.

Red-faced, I took my ice cream back behind a tree to eat it in privacy. There must be some powerful ingredient in ice cream. Even though it goes down cold, it warms you. Makes you feel people understand you and think you're a great fellow.

There were other tables selling plenty of good things to eat, every kind of pie imaginable – blueberry, lemon meringue, banana cream, apple, raspberry, peach, rhubarb – any of which you could have by the slice, so we did, three each. I decided on a piece of blueberry and a piece of peach and a piece of lemon meringue, and planned out in my mind just how I'd say it, and I said it just right. I don't think either Ernie or Harold even noticed, but I couldn't help grinning.

We decided to spend the last of our money on something to drink as we were all nearly parched. We were looking over the selection of drinks – orange crush, iced tea, lemon squash – when a fellow Harold knows told us they had birch beer up at the store on the other side of the hotel. We'd never had birch beer, but were willing to try anything. It tasted fizzy and some- what sour, but a lot of the lads and older men were drinking it so we joined them back behind the store. Ernie wiped his mouth and said, "This tastes awful. What's it made of?"

"Horse piss, from the smell of it," Harold said. Ernie handed the bottle to me, and I ended up drinking most of it to keep it from going to waste.

We recognized one or two of the men as local characters,

famous for leaning on their shovels instead of getting the ditches dug out. Some of them were drinking birch beer, but others were passing around a bottle of something probably stronger. We arrived in time to catch the tail end of a story.

". . . well sir, I tell ya, they never heard nothin' more of him from that day to this." The storyteller nodded at his audience, his foot propped up on a chopping stump at the edge of the group. "Neither hide nor hair of him was ever to be seen in these parts again."

"Got off the road into some swamp, likely, and couldn't get out," someone said.

"Doubt 'er." The man took a long pull from a dark brown bottle. "Sober a man as ever walked on two feet. Never once strayed from the road, so they say. Now this was long before my time or yours, mind you: sixty, seventy year ago, maybe eighty. People just startin' to settle in here. Wild as the back o' beyant."

A beak-faced man in a bowler hat said, "Drunk or sober, you'd be hard put to recognize the trail back in those days. I remember my grandfather telling about the way it twisted around swamps and in and out of the bush, and the track so broke up you never knew which way was right."

"Likely wolves got him."

We wedged ourselves into the circle, not to miss a thing.

"More likely bears."

"Coulda been just about anything back then. Back before the bridge was built."

"Most likely old John Oliver got him." This from a man with a sunburn on his face up as far as his eyebrows, and white from there to his hairline. I caught Harold nudging Ernie to look at me. I was listening so hard, I guess my mouth was hanging open. I took a long drink of the beer.

"Oliver! Ach-ptchoo!" An old man spat on the ground. Several others made the same comment. "Sure, nobody was ever able to pin a thing on Oliver. Slick as grease, he was."

The man with the white forehead said, "Maybe not, but they all knew what he was capable of. My pappy knew. Said old Oliver, in his day, was more devil than man. He used to say, 'Ferryman'll getcha if you don't come in the house.' He kept us lads in line with that for years. 'Ferryman'll getcha!'" He slapped his knee and guzzled his birch beer.

The bird-beaked man narrowed his eyes at the group. "If that old ferryman did halfa what he's accused of, sure he'da wiped out a goodly portion of the population of this and three other counties."

"All's I know," White Forehead said, "is they used to say, 'Never ask Oliver to take you 'crost the lake after dark. He won't do it, and it may be the worse for you.'"

"It's just made-up stories," said a stout man, younger than the others, trying without success to hitch himself onto the rail fence separating the store and the hotel. "Where's the proof?"

Bird-beak said quietly, "I hear Oliver's back." No one said anything for a moment.

"Whatcha say?" someone finally asked.

"Oliver's place is up for sale. Somebody lookin' to sell it, shack and all."

"Oliver's dead."

"How do you know?" There was a pause while the men scratched their heads and looked at each other, their eyebrows drawn together.

"Sure, it'll be the son, then."

"Son's dead."

Someone said, "Who's sellin' it, then?"

Bird-beak said, "Old geezer, old as Methuselah. I seen him."

Someone else piped up, "Oliver'd be damn near a hunert were he alive."

"Or more," someone added.

White Forehead said, "I say it's his ghost, and I say nobody's gonna spend good money on a place that's haunted by the devil hisself."

Somebody, an American by the sound of his voice, laughed heartily. "Haunted!" he said. "Well, I always heard tell this was as benighted a place as I'd ever see this side of the bogs of Ireland, but I never thought to hear grown men believin' in ghosts."

A few of the men took offense at this and moved up close to the stranger's face. The man with the white forehead said loudly, warding off a fistfight, "If boards and shingles could talk, that old shack of Oliver's could tell a gruesome tale or two. Myself, I saw the very print of the devil's hoof over there. And not too long ago, neither."

"Would have been a deer, surely."

"I believe I know deers from devils."

Bird-beak was looking over at us three boys. "The young lads, there, 'll be thinkin' this's all the gospel truth."

"So it is!"

An old man, who looked about a hundred himself, spoke in a voice that whistled and crackled like a crystal set, "Even if it was the full of the moon and you needed to cross the lake, you'da never got past his cabin, over there. You'da been a goner."

"And where are the bodies?"

"Could be anywhere," the old man whistled. "Don't believe it if you don't want, but most people know for a fact that if it was daylight, he'd take you, but woe betide you if the sun was gone down."

My ears were practically flapping by now, and so were Ernie's and Harold's, we were listening so hard. We'd heard bits and pieces of all this before now, but figured it was made-up. Bogeyman stories. Nobody had ever said exactly why you'd be a goner after dark, and I wanted to ask. I don't know whether it was the birch beer or the pie or the ice cream, but I was starting to feel mighty sure of myself, as if I could talk to anyone without a worry or a plan. I had another jolt from the bottle and said, "Why would-would-would-would-would." I sounded worse than ever.

The men stared at me and someone said, "Who's the woodpecker?"

I felt like punching him. I put down the bottle and lurched at him with my fists up, but Ernie grabbed me. I squirmed out of his grasp, but someone stuck out his foot and I tripped, landing headlong against the fence. I was dizzy for a moment and couldn't get my bearings. Ernie and Harold got on either side of me, pulling me away. I was shouting, "Let me at him! I'll murder the bum!" Well, I wanted to yell that, but I think I was just put-putting and sputtering like the *Bessie* boat's engine backfiring.

"Get some black coffee into him, lads, afore he goes home to Mama!" someone called after us. I was all for going back and breaking his jaw for him, but the two boys dragged me away back down to where the social was winding down. We could hear the band playing "Good night ladies, good night gentlemen." I wanted to stop to listen to them and dug my heels in. Ernie went off for coffee, and Harold stood near me ready to grab me if I started picking a fight.

But I wasn't in a fighting mood any longer. I was in a singing mood. "Merrily we roll along," I sang loudly to the accompaniment of the Smiths Falls band, "roll along, roll along, merrily we roll along, over the deep blue sea." People turned to look at me; some clapped; the band struck it up again, and I sang all the words perfectly without stuttering once. "Good night ladies," I sang, my voice ringing. "Good night gentlemen; good night everyone; it's time to say good-bye."

I could see Ernie making his way toward me, empty-handed. All the refreshment tables were closing down. I couldn't see Harold anywhere, but then I glimpsed him behind a stout woman, acting as though he didn't know me. "Merrily we roll along," I sang again. It was beginning to get dark. Fireflies winked like beacons. Bats swooped overhead among the tree branches. The crowd around the band was smiling at me, singing along, now. "Merrily we roll along," we all sang. I loved all those people just then. I especially loved one heavenly face surrounded by dark hair barely restrained by a ribbon. I smiled directly at her. Her lips parted and she stared back, puzzled, as if she knew me from somewhere. And then it hit me.

"Over the deep blue sea," I heard them sing as I darted behind the stout lady, yanking Harold along with me, fleeing to the boat. Ernie was right behind us. I nearly pitched headfirst into the boat while Harold untied it and Ernie grabbed the oars. "You get a bee up your drawers?" Harold asked me. "Why the sudden rush?"

"It was her," I said. "The girl from the row-row-row-row. This morning."

We rowed home in the dark without even a lantern. I had a bad taste in my mouth from the beer, and my head felt fuzzy. There wasn't much of a moon, but we could make out the shoreline well enough. We knew we weren't in any danger of running aground as there are few shoals between here and Sunnybank, not that far out, anyway. Here and there we saw dots of lantern light from a cottage – people sitting around a table playing cards or reading, I guessed – or a pale light weaving among the trees – someone on his way to the outhouse.

I wished I could escape from people altogether. Every time I got involved with strangers, I ended up looking like a fool. I never wanted to see that girl again.

Although she was good-looking.

Big eyes. She must have thought I was the type that went around terrorizing the ladies by diving at them stark naked and getting drunk and singing my lungs out. Well, I am, I guess, as far as she knows, anyway. All that dark hair, she has.

Pretty.

I always used to lump girls together as just "girls." Like cousin Ettie. I've never thought much about which ones are pretty. Ettie's pretty, too, I suppose, and Bessie, although she's only eight so it's hard to tell. Grandma says Auntie Min is pretty in her own way.

4

A Rafting We Will Go

(Today is my birthday.) This morning we carried water for the ladies to do the washing with. We then finished our job in the grove, and went fishing and sailing. Auntie Lizzie made an enormous cake for our supper and, after we ate it, we made a campfire near the tent and sat around it playing the mouth organ and singing with Ettie and Auntie Min and Mr. McAlpine, a friend of Ettie's, joining in. While we were having this revelry, the large steam yacht, Jopl, towing a barge loaded with cheese boxes, blew for the locks, and immediately we put out the fire and made a beeline for the locks. They let us get on, and we sat on the engine-room windows and watched the engineer at work. Both the pilot and

*the engineer were friendly and talked with us all
the way to the upper lock. They said they were
going to stay there all night, and asked us if we
wanted to go into Perth with them. They leave at
five o'clock in the morning.*

We got an alarm clock from the cottage to wake us up in time.
The cottage folk laughed at us and said the *Jopl* would be long
gone before we tumbled out of bed. We set the alarm for three
o'clock to be on the safe side. When it went off, I was in the
middle of a very realistic dream. Ernie fumbled with the clock
trying to turn off the alarm, but it wouldn't shut up until he
bounced it off the wall of the tent. We all just lay there.

"Come on," I said, finally, "we have to get up." I gave
them each an elbow in the back because it was my turn to
sleep in the middle. Harold kept on snoring on one side of me
and, on the other side, Ernie pulled the covers up over his
head and made a snarling sound like a cross dog.

Wedged in, I lay thinking about my dream and trying to
get back into it, but I couldn't. Probably just as well as I'm
trying to preserve my brain fluid. So I just lay there, thinking about things, about how I was officially sixteen now, and
would be out on my own before long. And then I got thinking about the hair I have growing out of my armpits and
growing someplace else that you're not supposed to think
about too much for fear of either turning into a moron or
getting slayed by God. This is what I heard anyway in the

senior boys Sunday school class from Mr. Lamb, our Sunday school teacher. He preached a sermon to us about somebody in the Bible who spilled his seed on the ground, and God slew him for it. I remember how all the boys started looking out of the corners of their eyes at each other, and Mr. Lamb said, "I know what you're thinking, you boys: that each of you has managed to escape the Wrath Of God, so far, but don't be too sure of yourselves. The Worst Is Yet To Come. Every time you have impure thoughts, if God does not Slay you outright, He has other ways of Meting Out Punishment. You will lose Brain Fluid. That's right boys, Brain Fluid." He told us that every time we waste our seed, we lose a portion of our brain fluid, and the more of it that escapes, the stupider we'll become until we turn into morons, unable to do the simplest sums or spell words like "cat." After this sermon, as soon as anyone did anything stupid, all the senior boys started laughing and pointing at the chap and saying, "What a moron!"

Usually me, unfortunately.

I hate thinking about morons so I crawled out over Harold, who tried to kick me in the ribs, but I was too fast for him. The other boys got up, finally, and we struggled into our clothes, all cold and clammy from the heavy dew during the night.

I got a fire going and we huddled over it, shivering while we waited for our porridge to cook and our eggs to boil. We were in plenty of time. The yacht had the steam up and the barge in place by 5:15, and we were soon underway. We sat in the engine room to keep warm until the sun got up, and asked a lot of questions about the operation of the engine.

If I had a boat like this, with sleeping quarters and a cooking galley, I'd explore all the bays and shoreline. I would search out every shoal and wedge permanent markers into them, so that people would know about the dangers ahead and could avoid them.

I went out to stand on the deck and watch the wildlife. A blue heron, frightened from his fishing spot, spread his ungainly wings and flapped away, with his legs behind him like bent sticks. "Grack! Rackafrack!" he swore at us. In the distance, gray ghosts of trees haunted the drowned lands until the sun, higher now, warmer, brushed them a honey color, bringing them to life just for the moment.

Ernie joined me and the two of us watched the passing scene. We saw a roof washed up against a ridge of land that reared up from the swamp like a dead body. "We should build ourselves a raft and go ex-ex-ex-exploring," I said. A raft would be better than risking damage to the bottom of one of Grandpa's boats.

Harold had come out and was leaning over the railing beside us. "What would we build it out of?"

"Logs," Ernie said, "and planks. There's lots of lumber at the carriage works."

"Unc-Unc-Uncle Will would never part with it. It's new stuff," I said.

47

Harold said, "Let's take it from that place up across from Rideau Ferry."

"What place?"

"You know, Oliver's place, that the men were talking about. It's going to be sold."

Ernie and I both looked doubtful.

"Why not?" Harold said. "Who would care? It'll probably just get torn down anyway, once it's sold." Neither Ernie nor I said anything. Harold looked right into our eyes. "You don't really believe it's haunted, do you?"

"No," I said.

"No," Ernie said.

"Then . . . ?"

"Harold, you can't just wal-wal-waltz across the lake and take s-s-s-someone else's property."

"It's an abandoned old shack. No one will care."

Ernie shrugged. I could see him starting to warm to the raft idea. Harold said, "We'll build a huge raft with sides on it and chairs, and take people for tours of the drowned lands and charge them a fare."

"No wait," Ernie said, "we could build a lean-to on it and live on it. Go where the breeze takes us."

"Why-why-why don't we ask the owner's permission, in-in-in case he objects?"

Harold gave me the kind of look you'd give Bessie if she asked a stupid question, although she usually never does. He said, "If you ask, they'll say no. If you just go ahead and do it, no one will be any the wiser. It's the way of the world, Freddie."

I know what Harold thinks: that I never take a risk, never make a move without a plan. But if I don't plan, I end up looking like a moron. I wish I could get a map made of my whole life. Then all I'd have to do is follow it.

By the time we got to Perth, Harold and Ernie had built a raft the size of a Spanish galleon, and I just kept nodding and saying things like, "Don't forget lace curtains on the windows," and "Maybe we should build runners in case the lake freezes over," and they said, "Nobody likes a wiseacre, Freddie."

The *Jopl* tied up in the canal basin in the center of town behind a lot of stores, with their fronts facing Gore Street and their backs facing the water. We helped unload the cheese boxes from the barge onto a wagon, and then set out to walk the short distance to Grandma's house. She and Auntie Ede were clearing up the breakfast dishes, and Uncle Will had already gone to work when we got there. Grandma insisted on giving us a second breakfast, which we didn't turn down.

We were scraping the last smear of egg yolk and the last crumb of toast down our gullets when the postman arrived. "Looks like a letter from your father," Grandma said, handing it to me. I placed it on the table, dreading its contents. *Frederick must pack up immediately*, it would say. *Summer is over forever. You've got a man-sized job in the city. I'm proud of you.*

"Well open it!" Ernie said. Instead I shoved it along to him and then leaned over his shoulder as he read out loud, "I hope you are all behaving in a mannerly fashion and not causing your relatives any undue anxiety." We looked at Grandma, whose expression seemed calm enough, so Ernie read on, "I have been thinking of paying a visit to that part of the country so you will not be surprised if I appear on your grandfather's doorstep. I have been developing an interesting plan, which I will explain when I get there, although that may not be for a fortnight as my assistant in the store is holidaying at the moment. In the meantime, Bessie is not to tease, Tom is not to be rough, and Ernie is to be helpful." He saved the last paragraph for me. "I hope Frederick is taking advantage of the outdoor life to build his character and to strengthen his nerves. I expect to see great changes in him."

Ernie still had the letter. "Interesting plan!" he said. "He might at least have given us more information." I took it from him and read it again myself to see if the "interesting plan" could in any way involve my lack of character and weak nerves.

Grandma said, "I think he misses you and doesn't want to admit it."

There was nothing in that letter to indicate that he missed us, and I thought I should set her straight. "He-he-he wants to ch-ch-check on the state of my nerves with a surprise visit."

"There's nothing wrong with your nerves."

I glanced away from her. Grandma is fairly smart, I guess, but she always seems to miss the main point.

"You'll just have to surprise *him*, won't you?"

I shook my head. She believes things are simpler than they are. I sometimes wonder how she managed to raise all her children and not learn anything about human nature in the process. Nothing I could do could possibly surprise my father.

After breakfast we went along the street to the carriage works and poked around the shop looking for old bits of wood to scavenge until Uncle Will kicked us out. Before we left, I managed to have a word with him. "Wh-wh-when will you teach me to drive the *Bessie*, Uncle W-W-W- . . . ?"

"One of these days," he said, "when the time is ripe." This is his usual line. I guess I looked disappointed because he shook his head at me. "You kids, you want everything immediately. Well, listen, you have all summer ahead of you, all your childhood ahead of you, all your long life ahead of you."

So he thinks. I sometimes wonder if he was ever a boy himself. Maybe Grandpa put him to work at the age of three, and he's been forced to be a man ever since.

We walked back to Grandma's, who collared us to do a few errands for her. Walking the sun-filled streets, we breathed in the civilized smell of freshly cut grass, and felt lonesome for the zesty pines and the fishy shore and the smell of the lake evaporating on our arms and backs. We bought some postcards for Tom and Bessie and wandered around town feeling like tourists, watching the men steam drilling and blasting for the new sewerage pipes until it was time to go back to the basin. The *Jopl* had its steam up by the time we arrived, our arms filled with supplies from Grandma: fresh bread for all, and a sticky bun just for us campers.

It was mid-afternoon by the time we got back to the upper locks. There were several boats ahead of us. "Ain't in a rush, I hope, for it'll take a while," a man rowing a large skiff called up to the pilot of the *Jopl*. "There's some kind of fuss down at the lower lock."

"Let's go see," Ernie said. We jumped ashore, thanked the captain for our ride, and pitched our supplies under a tree. We ran down to the lower lock where Mr. Buchanan, the lockmaster, had locked in a small rowboat operated by a white-haired old man crouched over his oars. The sluice gates were open; the water was rising. It swirled and eddied, pushing the boat this way and that. Up on the walk rail, Mr. Buchanan called down through a megaphone: "Grab the chain! Hold on to the chain!" But the man didn't seem to see the chains hanging down the stone wall, placed there to steady the boats. He didn't seem to know he was in a lock at all because he kept trying to use the oars, crashing time and again into the high stone walls, nearly capsizing.

We could hear the old man yelling something like, "Get away from me! I'm warning you! Help!" He let go of the oars to shield his head as if he were being attacked. Then he loosened one and brought it down with a crack on the side of the boat. "There!" he yelled. "There's an end of it!" He became calmer then and sat with his face in his hands.

At that moment a younger man appeared on the lock wall.

"Grandfather!" he called down, but the old man ignored him, or didn't hear him, and began thrashing about with his oar again, hitting at something or someone unseen.

Mr. Buchanan called across to the younger man, "I'm taking him back down again." To us he called, "Some of you lads come over here to the other side in case he drifts over."

We were not very eager to have our heads whacked by an oar, but we did as we were told and ran across the walk rail. Mr. Buchanan soon had the lock water back down to the level of the lake and, as he opened the gates, the old man seemed to get his wits back. He rowed himself out and brought his boat alongside the wharf opposite us on the other side of the channel, where his grandson grabbed the bow. "He gets confused sometimes," the younger man called up to Mr. Buchanan by way of explanation. "He has delusions. He's all right, now." We all stared at the younger man knowing we'd seen him before, but where, we didn't know. We stayed around long enough to see the young man help the old one into a boat something like the *Bessie* and tow the older man's boat up the lake toward Rideau Ferry.

"Poor old fella," Mr. Buchanan said. "Daft as a loon."

After supper Beaver Camp held another campfire on the point down near our tent. Tom was not put out about our trip to Perth aboard the steam yacht as he doesn't like getting up early anyhow. We sang for a while. Auntie Lizzie said I have the most musical voice of all the boys. I guess I like to sing because it's the only time I can be sure of getting the words out right.

Ettie and Auntie Min didn't come down because they're in a row over Ettie's friend Mr. McAlpine. Auntie Min thinks he's too old to be forcing his attentions on Ettie, and Ettie says she would be delighted not to have someone minding her business for her constantly. Auntie Lizzie mutters things under her breath like "Moses 'n Aaron" or "Heaven help us."

Grandpa said he would join us if someone would be kind enough to carry a chair down for him. So we had quite a little crowd, anyway, for our entertainment. Bessie started clamoring for him to tell a ghost story, and Grandpa said he didn't know any. Bessie kept insisting he did so. "Well," he said at last, "the nearest thing I can think of would be the dark and dirty deeds of old John Oliver." We older boys groaned because we'd already heard all that bogeyman stuff.

Tom told us to shut our traps and begged Grandpa to tell it anyway. "And make it the worst story you know," Bessie chimed in, and Grandpa was soon rubbing his hands together, ready to curdle our blood with tall tales.

"Now, don't you dare scare them, Father," Auntie Lizzie broke in. "These smaller ones won't sleep a wink."

"Oh, well, perhaps you're right," Grandpa nodded. He sat there with his arms crossed and his lips shut tight, looking off into the distance as if he had the satisfaction of knowing something gruesome, which we poor suckers would never find out.

"What kind of dirty deeds, exactly?" Bessie asked. She was encouraging a furry caterpillar to walk along a stick, prodding it every so often with her finger. Cross-legged beside her, Tom leaned over his knees and urged, "Come on, Grandpa! Tell!"

"How about some popcorn?" Auntie Lizzie said to change the subject. She had an old fire-blackened saucepan, with a lid and a long handle. She knelt down near the circle of stones surrounding the fire and set it right onto the coals.

Harold said, "Tell the story after Tom and Bessie go to bed. We campers can take anything."

"No fair," Tom said. "We can take anything, too, except for Bessie. Bessie had better go to bed." I waited for Bessie to give him a thump, but she was busy with her caterpillar.

The corn began to erupt like fifty guns and, after a moment, Auntie Lizzie pulled it away from the heat with a pot holder. Soon we were digging our paws into it and cramming it into our mouths. Bessie put some in her skirt, which formed a little dip, so that she could eat the pieces one by one. Beside her, Tom twitched and shook his shoulders and tried to reach his back to scratch it. We knew we were going to get a story, sooner or later. Whether truth or fiction depended on Grandpa's imagination. So between mouthfuls, we encouraged him to make it a good one and not hold anything back.

"Well," he said, starting off mildly, "I'll tell you this much. People say Oliver was a murderer, but he was never caught and the bodies were never found."

Tom leapt up at this announcement, dancing up and down, reaching down his back, pulling at his shirt.

"Mercy!" Auntie Lizzie said, pulling him away from the fire. "You've given the lad the fits!" The rest of us ignored him, and pretty soon the caterpillar fell out.

"Who did Oliver murder?" Harold asked. "And why didn't they catch him? And when did it happen?"

"How did they know it was Oliver?" Ernie asked.

I said, "How-how-how do they know there was a murder if they didn't find a body?" Grandpa was going to have to come up with some fancy storytelling to keep us sharpshooters interested.

He sat there pulling on his whiskers, his eyes roving over us, back and forth, reveling in our curiosity and our skepticism. It was obviously too much for him. In spite of Auntie Lizzie's protests, he leaned forward over his stick and said in a loud whisper to Tom, "Old John Oliver was the wickedest man ever to live in the county of Lanark." Tom shrank back but sat board straight, glued to Grandpa's every word. "Dead these many years, he is, but his infamy lives after him. A bogeyman if ever there was one."

I glanced around the campfire. The rest of us were sitting hunched over our knees, eyes bright. Tom and Bessie were hardly breathing, hardly daring to crunch down on the popcorn, not wanting to miss any part of the grisly tale. Ernie and Harold caught my glance and leaned back on their elbows, grinning sheepishly.

"Back in the days of the early settlers, back before the Rideau Canal was even built," Grandpa began, "there was only one route overland for people on foot or horseback from the St. Lawrence River to the town of Perth, and that was through bush so dense and dark and ahowl with wolves you'd swear it was the gates of hell, and wish it was, 'cause you'd know at least where you'd got to. And swampland so thick with mosquitoes and black snakes and all manner of slithering creatures that if you were a traveler, you'd wish you could lie down and die and get it over with. And if you ever found your way out to the banks of the Rideau, wild with the heat and the bug bites and the fear of having the flesh torn right off your bones, the first thing you'd see was the devil incarnate in the person of old John Oliver, standing with his back to his ferryboat and his hands on his hips, just awaitin'.

"And, oh, he was a sight indeed! A mean-lookin' beast of a no-neck man, his eyes raw and red, and scarcely a tooth in his slavering mouth. And if it was broad daylight, and after he'd seen your money, he'd set about with the help of his son – a younger version of himself – and together they'd get you and your horse and cart onto a raft the size of a barge. And together they'd ply oars made from the trunks of trees, one either side of the ferryboat, till at last you'd reached the other shore and could skee-daddle as fast as you could out of his sight. And that's the best that could be said.

"And the Rideau was not a lake to be sneezed at, either. Once the wind was up, tossing the waves as high as your head,

you'd think twice before attempting a swim across to avoid
the ferryman. No, sir, you were for it. It was the ferry or
nothing.

"'Ferryman,' you'd say, 'what will you charge to take me
across?' And if it was after the sun'd gone down, he'd answer,
'There's no coin big enough to tempt me out on the water
after dark.' And you'd say, 'I've half a crown with your name
on it if only you'll ferry me and my goods across the lake for
it may be late, but there's a full moon.'

"'You must bide with me this night,' he'd say. 'The wife,
there, likes a bit of company and she's cooked up a fine pot
of vittles. You'll get a soft bed and an early start in the
morning.'

"And if you were smart," Grandpa said, "you'd hie yourself out of that place as fast as your legs would carry you and
take your chances with the wolves until dawn, for if you were
weary and yielded to the ferryman's invitation, you'd never
again see the light of day."

"Why not?" Bessie said. She had wriggled herself a little
closer to Grandpa and was staring up at him.

Grandpa paused to light his pipe. At last he said in a loud
whisper, bending over Bessie, "He liked the taste of blood, so
they say."

"Now that's enough, Father," Auntie Lizzie said. Bessie sat
back, huddling close to Tom.

Grandpa's whisper grew deeper. "He liked to skewer a
man with an icepick and watch him squirm."

"Father!"

"And his missus, sure she'd slit a man from stem to gudgeon and rip out his innards to cook up for the next unsuspecting traveler."

"That's it! Bessie! Tom! Off to bed with you!" Auntie Lizzie was on her feet. She had Bessie by the arm and Tom by the collar of his shirt, but neither one was cooperating.

"I'd fight back," Tom said, wriggling free. "I'd grab the icepick and jab it into him, so I would." He happened to be standing beside me and pounded an invisible icepick into my shoulder. "Then I'd run out the door and swim across the lake."

"You wouldn't be strong enough," said Bessie, ducking under Auntie Lizzie's arm. "Besides, you can't swim."

"Can so."

"Cannot. Don't lie." She crouched at Grandpa's knee again. "What I'd do," she said, "is I'd trick him. I'd tell him someone was at the door and, as soon as he opened it, I'd run out and hide in a tree."

"What if he tied you up first?" Tom asked her. He'd found a length of string in his pocket and was winding it around his fingers to start a ball.

"Cut it out, you kids." This was Ernie. "What I want to know is, how do you know all this, Grandpa?"

"Very good question," Auntie Lizzie said. "Your grandfather likes nothing better than to take some bit of gossip, true or not, embellish it beyond all recognition, and then spew it out for the benefit of your young ears. Remember, first and foremost, he's a storyteller. Take heed."

"Oh, I'm not making it up. People knew, all right. They passed on stories from father to son and so on. Sure they say you could hear the screams clear across the lake. But people 'round here were scared of him. If you asked questions, chances were good that you'd end up in the stew pot yourself. I think there was an investigation at one time, but the local constabulary didn't turn up a thing."

Auntie Lizzie broke in, "Do you see my point?"

Grandpa pursed his lips, nodding at his daughter. "Well, I'm telling you the truth. If somebody's relative went missing, by the time they rounded up enough brave souls to get up a search posse, no track nor trail was left of the person. Gone. Vanished.

"And Oliver, there, he and his family always had the best that money could buy. The son rode a fine horse, and the missus had gold bangles and baubles like she was wife to a duke, more than what could ever come of a ferryman's pittance. And whether there were other offspring, I don't know. They'd have disappeared long before now, for no man alive would admit to being the son of old John Oliver. Even to this day people hereabouts look askance at strangers and wonder, *Now who would that fella's father be do you s'pose?*"

I asked. "But what-what-what happened to Oliver?"

"Murdered," Grandpa said. Our mouths all hung slack. That part we hadn't known.

"And his son?"

"Murdered, the two of them. They disappeared, at any rate. The wife, they say, died of natural causes. And not till then did travelers and local homesteaders dare to breathe the word 'safe.'"

I said, "Ol-Ol-Oliver's place is for sale." Harold nudged me with his foot and both he and Ernie stared at me, giving me the evil eye, willing me not to reveal their plan of liberating the lumber from Oliver's shack.

"Is it?" Grandpa said. "Been abandoned for years, of course. The house should be torn down before it falls on someone, not that anyone goes near the place. Some long-lost relative selling it, no doubt. Good luck to them. It's a blot on the landscape."

"Bessie and Tom!" Auntie Lizzie said in the lull while we contemplated the past. "It's long past your bedtime." Tom scrambled up without much fuss, but when Bessie was at last hauled to her feet, we heard the sound of cotton ripping, and Bessie let out a screech loud enough to make the entire Oliver family sit up in their graves. Tom had tied the skirt of her dress to the bush behind her. He took a running start toward the cottage with Bessie in her petticoat hot on his heels. Auntie Lizzie said something under her breath, bunched up the remains of the skirt, broke the string, and lumbered off after them. "You kids are the absolute limit," we heard her say. "Wouldn't I just like to tan your hides!"

5

If Music Be the Food of Love

Today the Perth Masons ran an excursion on the Rideau King away up the lake about 25 miles from our locks to the village of Newboro, with about 300 merry excursionists. We ran up when we heard it blow for the locks, and met about 50 men and boys who had got off the steamer at the upper locks to walk down to the second locks. Among them was a man we knew, who told us how to get a free trip to Newboro. They never ask to see your tickets from the time you get on in Perth till the time you get off again, he said. There's no return tickets. Anyone could get on either here or at Newboro, and the stewards would not know but what they came from Perth in the first place. So the three of us hustled to the

*cottage and got permission to go. In about two
minutes we had our Sunday clothes on. We
grabbed our change purses for fear of having to
pay after all, made a beeline for the locks, and
made it just as the boat got in. We mingled with
the men and boys who had walked down and
when they got on, we got on too, which meant
we were each 60¢ ahead.*

The *Rideau King* is a real beauty, three decks all painted
white, with a canopy over the stairs going up to the saloon
deck. At night, the whole thing is lighted with electricity and
heated by steam.

Most of the men and boys were either down below or up
on the hurricane deck, where the Perth Citizens' Band provided lively entertainment with their clarinets and their
cornets and their trombones. Most of the women and small
children were on the saloon deck in between, where, besides
staterooms, there were men's and ladies' toilet rooms with hot
and cold running water. The people on the saloon deck had
the benefit of a piano and violin playing in the background.

We made a stop at Rideau Ferry, pausing just long enough
to pick up a few more passengers. Pacing back and forth on
the government dock, with parasols, wicker baskets, and
folding camp stools, were a party of six or eight people
waiting to board the *Rideau King*. A young woman tipped up
her parasol to look up at the boat, and something went thump

inside my chest. There she was again – the girl with the hair. And the eyes. I felt two sensations at once. I wanted to leap over the farside of the boat and swim for the opposite shore, but at the same time, I had this huge urge to hold out my hand and help her aboard and to say to her, *This is the real me.* She would see how my hair was slicked smooth, and how gallant and handsome I was in my Sunday jacket and tie. I would say, *Would you like to dance?* The music sounded like a waltz, filtering down from the saloon deck as if from some heavenly source.

And she'd say, *With pleasure.* And she'd smile up at me, and I'd take her in my arms and . . .

"Holy mackerel!" Ernie said. "Isn't that that girl?"

"What girl?"

"You know."

Harold said, "Of course it is. She looks kinda stunned as if she's still in a state of shock."

"She doesn't look-look-look stunned." Actually she looked incredibly beautiful.

"Look at those two men with her!" Harold said.

Her dress, blue with white here and there, showed off her figure, which was slender and, I think, tall.

"Look!" Ernie said, "The madman at the locks the other day! And the other fella, the one we've seen before, some-where."

Beside her, waiting for the excursion boat to ease against the wharf, was the man who was becoming a familiar sight around these parts. Not only had he been at the locks a few days ago with the old man, but Ernie was right, he had been the girl's companion in the rowboat that unforgettable morning. I now recalled it clearly.

"The old fellow seems all right now," Harold said.

I must admit there was something about the younger man I didn't like. Maybe it was the long, full mustache he seemed so proud of, the way he kept stroking it. He was guiding the girl by the elbow up the gangway in a chummy way, although he looked older than she was by at least ten years. Then he turned to assist the bent, old, white-haired man, his grandfather, who was right behind her. The girl wore a wide-brimmed hat, which shaded her face and partially hid her bouncing hair tied back with a blue ribbon. Once the party was aboard, she called something to her friends – another girl and some older women – and began to climb the stairs. Behind her, the old man, his back bent into a capital C, heaved himself upward, step-by-step, pausing every so often to catch his breath.

As the *Rideau King* eased away from the dock, we saw the bridge master crank open the swing bridge. It slid slowly over the water until the gap was wide enough to allow us passage through to Big Rideau Lake. Our steam billowed from the huge smokestack, and our whistle sounded deep and mellow as we saluted other boats on the lake. "Let's go up," I said, once the new arrivals were out of sight.

Harold said, "Don't you think she's seen just about enough of you already?" He and Ernie nearly split their bellies laughing while I stared coldly in the other direction, thinking about icepicks and their many uses. I said, "She did-did-didn't even see me that morning. The sun was in her eyes."

"The sun wasn't even up," Harold gasped, holding his sides.

"I'm-I'm-I'm going to the top deck. There's a better view." I strode to the stairs and took them two at a time.

The view was magnificent. I tried to lose myself in it and forget about my embarrassing moments. We steamed past meadows scattered with stones thick as pumpkins and, here and there, cows and horses bent their necks to drink from the lake. Among the reeds, ducks groomed themselves or turned tails up, hunting for food. We saw several cottages hidden among tall pines, but as we progressed, much of the shoreline remained unpopulated. About twenty minutes into the trip, coppery rose-hued rocks reared up from the lake against the shore, battling with dense forest for space. A bent cedar grew up from a deep crevice in the rock face, staking its claim in the world against all odds and I thought, there's character for you.

Ernie and Harold finally climbed to the top of the boat to join me. We were in the Rocky Narrows now, the deepest part of the lake at three hundred feet. Two fishermen in a rowboat wrestled with an enormous catch: a lake trout, it looked like, or landlocked salmon as they're called around here. It splashed above the surface, fighting for its life. We scurried to the back of the boat to see what would happen when our swells hit their skiff broadside. Cunningly, the man played out his copper line, letting the fish think he was home free while the boat bobbed and dipped in our wake. The minute they were stable, he began to reel him in, giving him just enough slack, now and then, to keep him interested. With the help of his chum wielding an oversized landing net, they managed to get the monster over the gunwale and into the boat. The men on our deck sent up a cheer, and our captain gave a blast on the steam whistle. The men held up their trophy as best they could – twenty-five pounds, I'd wager, if it was an ounce.

I made a big show of being absorbed by the antics of the fishermen, but all the time I had one eye on the deck below, where the girl and her friends sat in deck chairs or leaned against the railing. The girl, one elbow propped on the railing, seemed to say, *Oh!* and put her fingers to her lips as the fishermen landed their catch. She turned and smiled at her companion, the man with the drooping mustache, and laughed at something he said.

After the excitement of the fish, people left the rail to walk about the boat. She took off her hat and rested her back against the rail, spreading her arms along its length and turning her face up to the sun. If her hat should happen to escape and fall into the lake, I would dive from the top deck and swim after it. Carrying it in my teeth, I would climb aboard again and, as I presented it to her, I'd make a deep bow, and she would say, *You are the most valiant boy, I have . . . I mean . . . man I have ever met.*

She looked up toward our deck just then, shielding her eyes against the sun, and I retreated to the side rail feeling like a romantic fool.

In almost no time, it seemed, we had wound our way among the many islands – some with cottages on them, some as wild-looking as they'd been since the beginning of time – dotting the broadest part of the lake. We gave wide berth to the shoals. I think about shoals a lot. I even dream about them, always the same dream: I'm in a boat something like the *Bessie*, flying along through the water, never really feeling secure, not knowing when I might run against a submerged shoal. Suddenly one appears, lurking just beneath the surface of the water. And I have this sense that it was meant to be there, waiting for me. It gleams a menacing yellow where the light pierces it through the water, yet I'm helpless to change my course. I tense myself, waiting for the crunch of metal propeller and the splintering of wood against solid rock, but it never happens. At least, not so far. The water's always just deep enough to let me sail over it unscathed, and I wake up feeling grateful and lucky. The feeling doesn't last, of course. There probably is a shoal out there that will destroy my boat someday.

People began opening their picnic baskets, and spreading napkins on their knees. We were getting close to the Narrows Lock, which would admit us to the Upper Rideau. Off in the distance we could see Foley Mountain, a high crest of land that loomed above the village of Westport. My stomach rumbled. We hadn't had time to pack a lunch – our punishment, I guess, for being stowaways. "I'm going down to the bottom deck to see if I can-can-can buy something to eat," I said to Ernie. He and Harold decided to save their money for Newboro, our destination.

I stood in line at a counter where they were selling bags of peanuts in their shells, licorice drops, peanut brittle, and lemonade. Peanuts were the cheapest so I practiced the word in my head until it was my turn. Just then an assistant joined the man behind the counter, and the queue behind me split in two. And there, suddenly, was the girl, beside me, her purse open, waiting to ask the assistant for something. I felt my neck and ears burning. I knew I was staring at her, rudely, but couldn't stop. The man behind the counter was saying to me, "Yes, sir, what can I get you?" She looked straight at me then, and I made a huge effort to move my eyes. The man had both hands planted on the counter, his face pushed straight into mine, waiting for me to make my purchase. I tried to say "peanuts" the way I'd rehearsed, but my lips got twisted and wouldn't cooperate. I knew my eyes were blinking like signal lamps, and my Adam's apple was wobbling up and down, and all I could say was, "Pea-pea-pea-pea."

"Toilets are one deck up, buddy," the man said, and all the people around me chuckled. I wanted to sock him, bloody his nose. And I hate to say it, but the other thing I wanted to do was cry. Just wail, the way I used to when I was a little kid and something like this would happen and my mother would pull me in tight against her hip and twist her fingers around in my hair and I'd feel better, as if somebody was on my side, for once. And my father would say, *Don't spoil the lad like that. He's got to learn to speak up.*

I didn't wail. I didn't even run away, although I should have, maybe. Instead, I went right on making an ass of myself, my neck stretching out of my collar like a turtle's, my chin moving up and down as I finally spat out, "Nuts."

"Good lad," the fellow said, and fetched me down a bag of peanuts. "No charge, buddy," he said in a voice that sounded like a pat on the head. He looked at me in a kindly way as if I were some kind of a poor, brainless nincompoop. I slapped a nickel on the counter, took the damn peanuts, and elbowed my way out of the crowd without looking at anyone, cramming the hateful bag into my coat pocket.

I stood by myself in the stern end of the boat leaning against the rail, staring down at the white water churning out behind, saying to myself, *So what, it doesn't matter*, and all the time, some other voice in me was saying, *Yes, it does*. I felt like flinging myself overboard and drowning just to spite the fellow. But then I remembered I was a pretty strong swimmer so I'd end up bobbing along in the wake of the boat. Playing the fool, as usual.

"I have a feeling I've met you somewhere before." She appeared beside me, her hair blowing across her face. She had a bag of peanuts in one hand and was trying to push her hair

70

back with the other, but a strand caught on the corner of her lip when she smiled and I wanted to brush it away for her. But I didn't. I stood up straight, trying to make myself as tall as she was, but I think she had a few inches on me. I shook my head in answer to her question. "D-d-d-don't think so," I said.

"You look awfully familiar." She opened her bag of peanuts and took one out. She placed the bag on the railing while she cracked the shell. "Want one?"

I pointed to my bulging pocket and left it at that. Maybe I could develop my own sign language, I was thinking. The silence between us felt as tense as it does sometimes if you're in church, for instance, and you drop a silent but deadly rose because you can't help it, and you hope everyone will think someone else caused the stink because it's so embarrassing. Standing in the stern of the *Rideau King* with this beautiful girl wasn't exactly like that, but the lack of words was every bit as embarrassing. There were lots of things I could have said, like, *Lovely day*, or *What a fine excursion*, but I felt too low to even try. I pulled out my watch, glanced at the time, and put it away again. I didn't even tell her the time.

After we'd stood there staring at the water for about three days she said, "Don't be downhearted. I know a man who has a stammer something like yours and he ended up in the House of Commons. When it comes to making a speech, he told me once, he can get the words out just as slick as you please. And as for the rest of the time, he simply pretends he's making a speech. He clears his throat, pictures himself at a podium, and thinks to himself, *Ladies and gentlemen*. Out loud he says things like, 'What an extraordinarily fine day,' just to test himself on difficult words. It seems to work, although I wouldn't necessarily recommend it. It makes him sound like a pompous ass."

I stared at her. She was grinning at me with all these dazzling teeth showing, and her eyes sparkling as if she liked to shock people. I found myself grinning back. I have to admit I *was* a little bit shocked. I'd never heard a girl talk so freely and I'd never heard a girl say "ass."

She stuck out her hand, just like a man, and said, "I'm Nora Maberly." Her hand felt small and firm and cool in mine, and reluctantly I let it go again.

"Fr-Fr-Fr-Fred Dickinson," I managed to get out.

"Pleased to know you," she said, and just as she did, her elbow bumped her bag of peanuts, knocking them overboard.

"Blast!" she said, "Now that was silly of me."

I began tugging on my bag of peanuts, trying to keep the bag from ripping, trying to get my fingers around it, trying to get it out of my pocket where it was securely wedged, and thinking, I'll tear the pocket right off the coat with my teeth if I have to. They burst free, half of them spewing all over the deck, but enough remained in the bag that I could offer them to her.

"Why don't we share them?" she suggested. We sat down beside each other on a bench at the back of the engine room and cracked shells. I threw a peanut up in the air and it came down in my mouth. She tried it then, but it bounced off her shoulder. She tried again, but her aim was way off, so I ducked close to her and caught it myself, which made us both laugh. Kind of childish, maybe, but it was exciting when our shoulders touched. She acted pretty young, but she could have been as old as Ettie. Hard to say.

She was telling me about the people she was with. The white-haired gentleman was an old family friend, and the younger man, Wilf, was his grandson. I wanted to ask her more about this Wilf, such as, why didn't he drop dead and what was he to her, but I didn't trust myself to get the right words out. Of the other people, one was her sister, one was her mother, and the others were friends of her mother's. They had all come down from Ottawa where they live, and were staying for the month of August at Hotel de Coutts, which is what people from the city call the hotel at Rideau Ferry. We call it the Coutts House.

I spotted Ernie and Harold just then, coming around the corner of the engine room. When they caught sight of me sitting with *that girl*, they stopped in their tracks. I thought their eyes would roll like marbles right out of their sockets onto the deck. I pretended not to see them, and they immediately picked up their feet and marched backward around the corner, out of sight.

"Who were those boys?" she asked.

"Dunno," I lied. I felt a flush rise over my neck, giving me away.

"Yes, you do," she teased, "you just don't want to tell me."

A shadow fell across us and when we looked up, there was Wilf, arms folded across his chest, blocking the sun, pink lips smirking at us beneath his droopy mustache. "Well, Nora, we were all wondering whether in your boredom you'd decided to jump overboard."

She got to her feet a little too abruptly to suit me, and briefly introduced us. "Wilf, meet Fred." I stood up, too, to shake hands with him, and a cold and clammy handshake it was. "You'd best come back to the fold, my dear," he said to Nora. "Your mother, as usual, is becoming worried about you."

I watched him take her arm, gripping it as if he owned it, guiding her back toward the stairs. He leaned over her and I heard him say, "Don't we know that chap from somewhere?" I couldn't hear her reply, but she did turn back to wave at me, and I'm not certain about this, but I have a strong feeling that she winked.

We got to Newboro wharf by about 1:17 and, as our crowd disembarked, the village's brass band escorted us uptown. We walked around viewing the principal streets for a while, but were soon attacked by pangs of hunger, which we soothed with ice cream and chocolates. Although this kind of a lunch was not very strengthening, it suited us perfectly.

Ernie and Harold didn't waste much time getting out of me how I ended up sitting with *that girl*. "At least do-do-do her the courtesy of calling her by her name."

"Which is?"

"Nora."

"No-o-o-ra," Harold crooned. We were walking along the shady side of the main street, licking chocolate off our fingers and wiping our mouths on our coat sleeves. "No-o-o-o-ra, when you sleep you sno-o-o-o-ra, I can hear you through the do-o-o-ra."

"Shut up," I said.

"Even through the flo-o-o-ra."

"Cut it out. Nora's one-one-one of the nicest names in the English language," I said.

"Oh-oh! I think I smell a love affair coming up."

"Harold, s-s-s-suck eggs!"

We had reached the agricultural grounds, where a baseball game between the Perth team and a team from nearby Elgin were battling it out. Just ahead of us, about to take a seat in the covered bleachers, was the white-haired gentleman – Nora's friend – the grandfather of beastly Wilf. He was leaning heavily on the arm of another man, no one I'd ever seen before.

"Let's go take-take-take a load off our feet," I suggested, heading for the bleachers.

"Move down," Harold said after we'd climbed in, but I shook my head. I wanted to be right where I was, directly behind the old gentleman. I thought I might overhear him say something interesting about Nora, or something incriminating about Wilf – Wolf, as I was beginning to think of him. We all took off our suit coats to let the sweat dry on our shirts. I was thinking of Bessie just then. She'd be holding her nose if she were with us. It was a relief to get out of the late-afternoon sun for a few minutes.

"You can hardly see the game past that idiot standing up down there," Harold complained. "Let's move farther in."

The idiot standing up, taking a huge interest in the game, was Wilf. He glanced over his shoulder at his grandfather, but didn't come back to join him. I was leaning forward now, tilting my head, trying to catch what the two men a couple of rows below us were talking about. I put a finger to my lips to shush Harold. Out of the corner of my eye I saw someone hit a home run. Perth was apparently winning.

The old man said something, but I couldn't make it out because people were cheering the home run. He had a low, rasping voice. I heard the other man say loudly into his ear, "It's a little late in the day to change your mind."

The old man gave a wheezing cough. "What did you say?" His companion repeated what he'd said. The old fellow chewed on his teeth for a moment. "Nothing's signed. No money's changed hands. I think you might consider granting an old man his dying wish." He turned woebegone eyes to his companion's face.

The other man started lighting a cigar, drawing on it as the match flared, turning his head to let the smoke out between his teeth, giving us the full benefit of it. Ernie wrinkled his nose and Harold coughed, but I rather liked it. Wilf was making his way toward the two men. I bent over to retie my bootlace so he wouldn't see my face and recognize me.

"What seems to be the problem?" I heard him ask.

The cigar-smoking man said, "You know I offered to buy the whole parcel of land off your granddaddy fair and square. No stipulations. And now he says he won't sell the waterfront, where the building is. The rest of the land's not worth a bent dime. It's all swamp and where it's not swamp, it's rock. Enough rock there to sink half a continent. It's worthless."

The old man said to Wilf, "You can sell the rest of the land the very day I die, if you want, but until then, the cabin on it remains untouched or else the deal's off."

Wilf bent toward his grandfather, nodding, agreeing, then stepped closer to the other man. "He's an old man," he said quietly. I glanced up long enough to see him give the other man a quick wink. "He doesn't know what he's saying."

The grandfather scowled up at Wilf. Deaf as he was, he'd heard that. "Don't I, though?" he said.

The man puffed on his cigar for a moment, then said, "I've got a work crew set to go in there, once the deal's settled, to knock the building down and cart it away."

Ernie and I looked over at Harold. He didn't look worried; he looked as if he had a foolproof plan. He folded his arms and grinned as if the raft were built and waiting for us tied to Newboro wharf.

The old man rasped, "Call them off, then! When I agreed to sell it, I was in so low a condition I didn't think I'd live out the week. Certainly, I never expected to live long enough to see the place invaded."

"The cabin's not what you'd call a thing of beauty," Wilf said into the old man's ear. He was sitting down now, jiggling his knee up and down, his neck muscles taut.

"Don't I know it!" The old man wheezed out another cough and spat over the side of the bleachers onto the ground.

"What's it to you, anyway?" the other man asked. "I guess you inherited it from the original owners, but they're long dead. Folks around there would be glad to have the cabin leveled. They say it's haunted."

"Eh?"

"Haunted. It's an eyesore. People want it down."

"No doubt, no doubt." The old man got shakily to his feet muttering something about wretchedness and evil, but I couldn't hear him clearly. His lined face was the color of split wood, left to dry. "It's cursed," he growled, and a patch of color crept into his cheeks. "I know all about it. Gypsies won't go near it. Tinkers, tramps run from it, scared witless, they say. Oh, I know, I know." He closed his eyes for a moment, teetering on his feet. The other man stood up, too, and put out a hand to steady his bent frame. The old man shuddered and said hoarsely, "Dread! It washes over me sometimes, thick as pooled blood." He looked over his shoulder, fear in his eyes, seeing something we couldn't. "Running all my life," he whispered. "All my life!" His voice cracked with emotion. "Running away and I'm tired. Tired out." He was mumbling to himself now. "Running all my life. Yes, yes, yes. Where's wee Willie? I've lost him!" He stepped down shakily from the grandstand onto the rough ground.

Wilf shouted, "You're raving again, Grandfather!" To the other man he said, "You can't believe a word he says. His mind's going."

His grandfather turned eyes on Wilf that looked perfectly sane. "Eh? So you may think," he said. "The mind's a strange and private land." He stood where he was and twisted his neck to look up at the other man as best he could. "Listen to me," he said. "I'm asking you, and I'm begging you. Just allow me to be safe in my grave before you so much as draw out a nail or pull away a board."

Wilf was standing now, too, and the old man turned pleading eyes up to him. "It's all I ask." His plaintive voice rang out in spite of the game in the background. "Do we need the money that badly?"

Wilf shrugged. "As a matter of fact, we do, Grandfather, but it's whatever you say." Behind the old man's back he gave the other fellow a long-suffering look. In a low voice he said, "He'll come around." We watched the three of them walk together to the edge of the fairgrounds, shake hands, and part company. Wilf looked back at the other man, but the other man didn't turn around.

"What-what-what was that all about?" I asked. I was pretty sure I knew, but I wanted to hear some supporting statements.

"Our proposed raft, is what it was about," Harold said. "If we want lumber, we're going to have to act fast."

We left the fairgrounds, not having any particular ties to either team out on the playing field, and took the road back to the village. The sun was lower in the sky, but still scorching. "Are you sure he was talking about old Oliver's shack?" Ernie asked.

Harold said, "He wasn't talking about a brick privy."

"Maybe it really is haunted," Ernie said. "Maybe we should get our lumber somewhere else."

Harold snorted. "Haunted! Pull yourself together, Ernie-girl!" He turned his head, shaking it as if he couldn't believe his ears. Then he turned back fast and yelled, "Boo!" right in Ernie's face. Ernie obliged him by jumping about a foot off the ground, and Harold fell over laughing. I didn't know whether Ernie actually believed in ghosts, but it wouldn't have surprised me. He has a lot of fantastic stuff going on in his head that you'd never know about unless you paid attention.

Just to get Harold back to reality I said, "We can't tear-tear-tear it down with our bare hands."

"Why not? It's practically falling down anyway. But I tell you what, when that chap buys it and the workmen begin to knock it down, we'll come along and offer to lighten their load for them. That's simple enough, isn't it?"

It did sound simple the way Harold talked. He continued, "Let's say this is our secret project and no matter what, we'll keep an eye on the place by rowing past it every day until we see the workmen, and then nab all the boards we can get. Whataya say?"

If Ernie had any second thoughts, you couldn't tell. His face was like a wiped slate. "Count me in, I guess," he said.

I don't know what mine showed: that I was losing interest, maybe; that the plan sounded too much like a game a child might make up; that I had other things on my mind, like the shape of Nora's face, which was triangular, ending with a perky dent in her chin, and I sure wouldn't have minded seeing it one more time.

I started mulling out loud. "Why-why-why do you think the old fella didn't want the building torn down?" We were back now, on Newboro's main street, where both hotels flew banners welcoming the excursionists and inviting them to come in and enjoy a hearty supper.

"Who knows?" Harold said. "Who cares? He's just some old man."

We heard a deep steam whistle blow for the locks, and Harold and Ernie took off in that direction to have a look while I lagged behind a little, kicking a stone along in front of me. He's not just some old man. He's a man with a troubled past. I bet he knows things we can't even imagine.

The *Rideau Queen*, a bigger, statelier version of the *Rideau King*, was cooling her engines waiting to be locked through. We could see people strolling about on the upper decks. Once she was in the lock, we got talking to a deckhand, asking questions, showing a lot of interest. "Hop aboard," he said. "Take the grand tour."

We all shrugged as if it didn't matter whether we did or we didn't, but, grinning all over, we jumped aboard to ride as far as Newboro wharf. Although she didn't look much longer or wider than the *King*, the *Queen* had more rooms. We scurried all over her not to miss anything. The folks back at the cottage would want a full description of the staterooms, all bright with flowery coverlets on the beds, and the swanky dining room done up in polished wood and plate-glass mirrors. There were green plush chairs in the saloon and a green carpet to match and, up above on the hurricane deck, a snug smoking room with leather chairs and a grand view because the walls were just about all glass.

"Doesn't matter which boat you bought your ticket for, you can ride back with us, if you like," one of the stewards said. We looked at each other a little sheepishly, remembering that we hadn't bought tickets at all. The steward was saying, "We stop in at Westport and Portland on the way back."

"Let's do it," Harold said.

It was tempting because I like exploring new towns. On the other hand, there was Nora. I couldn't desert her. I pictured myself going straight up to her and offering my arm. I could see us strolling up and down the deck, talking, laughing, gazing into each other's eyes. No, we had to go back on the *King*. That's all there was to it. I said, "It'll make us pretty-pretty-pretty late getting back. Our folks might get worried." Ernie, yawning, sided with me and so Harold had to give in.

As evening fell and the time came to leave, we boarded the *King*. I looked back to where the *Queen* was moored, behind us, and there was Nora, the ladies she was with, the white-haired gentleman, and wolfish Wilf all set to board the *Queen*. I ran for the gangway, snaking through the press of people on our boat, hollering for Ernie and Harold to come with me, but we were too late. They'd pulled up the gangway, and we were already a few feet out from shore. I climbed up on the rail, figuring I could jump it, and was just about to when I was pulled backward. I landed in a heap at the feet of a steward. He'd just spoiled my chances of spending the evening with the only girl in the world for me.

I heard Harold say to the steward, "See, he can't help it. He's not right in the head and takes fits." He sounded so convincing I began to wonder if he was right. "But don't worry, we'll keep an eye on him for the rest of the trip."

When I looked up, people were backing away from me. Some of the ladies had their hands over their mouths and were pulling small children back out of my reach. Ernie was trying to yank me to my feet. I don't know what came over me, but I turned up my lip as if I was going to snarl and snap, and a few people gasped. I was roaring mad. I wanted to growl and lash out at anybody and everybody. If only that jackass hadn't pulled me back, I'd have sailed over the water and landed like an eagle back on the wharf. I would have bowed to Nora, and she'd have clung to my arm and smiled up at me. Well, not up, I guess. Smiled down at me? We'd have sat down on a nearby bench, shoulders touching, and smiled at each other.

I stood up and dusted off my clothes. We were far enough out from shore that I couldn't see Nora's face. She was probably laughing at me playing the clown. Or shaking her head, thinking, *What a moron*! Or looking horrified because what if I am some kind of actual madman? Like the old fellow? How would I know? You probably wouldn't know until the men in white coats came after you with a big net. I wished Nora could see what it's really like inside me. I'm only disguised as a fool.

Harold was glaring at me and I realized I was just standing there watching the *Rideau Queen* with all her decks lit up, and all the people filing aboard get smaller and smaller, and Nora's pink cheeks and bright eyes, which I couldn't even see now, but knew were disappearing once again, perhaps forever. I felt as lonely as if I had, by chance, fallen off the world and was watching it go on without me.

Harold nudged Ernie. "Ain't love grand?" he said.

"Wouldn't know," Ernie said. "Never been in it."

I ignored them both, straining my eyes for a last glimpse of Nora. I couldn't see her. She was probably smiling up at Wilf.

6

Two Steps Forward
and One Step Back

*It poured rain just before noon today, and owing
to the kindheartedness of the cottage folks, we
were not compelled to cook our own dinner.
Friends of Ettie's rowed over from across the
lake between cloudbursts, and we all spent the
afternoon playing* FLINCH *and* FAN TAN. *At
about three o'clock, it stopped raining. The girls
took Ettie and went off in their boat looking for
fun. Girls seem to require a lot of different
people around them all the time, which could get
on your nerves, in my opinion. Harold, Ernie,
Tom, and I went fishing. Ernie caught two bass,
and Tom caught a big mudpout.*

We go fishing or sailing nearly every day up past the Oliver shack, but so far no one has gone near the place to start tearing it down. Today we took Tom with us and just glanced at the property without saying a word. "Is that the place that's for sale?" Tom asked.

"Dunno," Ernie said.

"You do so," Tom said, giving us all a suspicious look.

I was teaching Tom how to clean fish down beside the boathouse where we have an old table just for that purpose. I think mudpouts are the ugliest creatures the lake produces, black with tentacle-like things hanging down like a cat's whiskers, which is why some people call them catfish. I had just finished cutting off the mudpout's wicked head. Tom stared doubtfully at the blood running along a crack in the table, disappearing through one of its many knotholes. I handed him the bone-handled knife, slick now with blood, to slit the fish's belly. He stood there with it for a moment or two, getting up his courage. It's not the pleasantest job in the world, but it's one you have to master if you insist on catching fish. Bessie wormed her way in beside Tom and said, "Too bad it's still alive."

"Is it?" Tom asked in alarm.

"Of course not," I said.

Bessie said, "Then why is it wagging its tail?"

Tom put down his weapon.

I said, "Fish don't wag their tails," and handed him back the knife. "Just make a nice-nice-nice deep cut all the way along its belly." He put the point gingerly against the fattest part of the belly and pressed lightly. "Stick it in," I said. He was about to plunge the knife in when the fish's tail gave a mighty flap against the bloody table, and Tom let out a shriek that brought Auntie Lizzie on the run from the cottage where she was cooking supper.

"Glory!" she yelled. "Is he stabbed?"

"He's fine," I called back. I grabbed the stick Bessie had pushed up through a hole in the table to manipulate the fish's tail, and threw it away. "Go help your auntie with the supper," I said. "This is no place for girls."

"But I like it," she said. "Let me stab one, too."

"We're not stabbing the fish; we're cleaning them."

Ettie and her friends appeared then rowing toward the boathouse. Bessie ran to catch their bow and help maneuver them into the boat slip beside the *Jumbo*. We could hear them chatting away, excited about something. "I wish I had my blue muslin with me," I heard Ettie say. "Last year there were no dances at all and I brought scads of clothes."

One of Ettie's friends said, "Trust those Maberly girls to stir things up. They're both high-steppers, especially Nora."

I think my body temperature rose about twenty degrees. Sweating, red-faced, I left Tom scowling into the fish's slimy innards and ducked into the boathouse. Bessie was tying the boat for them to a ring in the wall with about twelve knots, and Ettie and her friends were tucking up their dresses in an effort to climb out of the boat. I held out my hand to assist.

"You're all over fish, Freddie!" Ettie squealed, pulling back her hand. "Don't touch us." They tumbled out on their own while I wiped my hands on my pants, and one girl got the heel of her shoe caught in her dress and ripped it a little. "Oh, fiddle!" she said.

"I-I-I-I." I stopped. And they all stopped, standing there in the boathouse, waiting for me to spit out whatever it was I wanted to say. "H-h-heard you-you-you." They waited and then Bessie, as usual, came to my rescue.

"Is there going to be a dance?"

"Yes," Ettie said. "At Rideau Ferry."

Her friend Augusta said, "The Maberlys are having a private ball at the hotel next Saturday to liven up their summer holiday."

"How-how-how. Do-do-do."

Ettie let out a sigh, held her lips together, and waited. I know I'm a true test to her patience, but to give her credit, she always waits for me to have my say. I finally managed to ask how she knew the Maberlys. It turns out they've all known Nora Maberly and her sister, Edna, from the beginning of time, and have managed to keep her a secret from me. Ettie said, "If you boys would ever come socializing with us girls, you would be acquainted with lots of the young people around here, too. But no, you have to go off fishing or tooting about on barges. I don't know how you ever expect to have any fun in the summer." I listened to them blathering on about the Maberly girls. They agreed that Edna was the nice one, and Nora nice too, but a bit exotic (Ettie's word). A bit tempestuous (also Ettie's word).

Ettie said, "We saw them out in their boat this afternoon and they asked us to help them round up all the nice young people we could lay our hands on, as they want a large party." I stood there staring at Ettie, willing her to notice how nice I was, and how young yet mature.

"What are you looking so hopeful about?" Ettie asked.

I couldn't stop my eyes from blinking, I was so eager. "May I-I-I go?"

"Freddie," she laughed, "you can't even dance."

I suppose I must have shown her a long face because she patted my arm as she left the boathouse with her friends. I slouched against the door frame and watched them skip lightly up the path to the cottage, laughing, teasing each other. They just seem to glide along in their lives, not like me, lurching, stumbling over just about every second blade of grass. Ettie glanced back over her shoulder, then stopped and turned around. "I could try to teach you, I suppose – sometime when you're not quite so fishy." Her friends laughed and pulled her along with them, linking arms. I couldn't imagine Nora chumming with this giddy bunch. I imagined her alone, on a hill, holding her hat against the wind, her dress billowing, waiting for someone. Me.

The rain threatened to make a comeback just as we Beaver Camp boys got our supper cooked and our table set. The sky, black now as tarnished pewter, had taken on a yellowish glow around the edges, which meant not just rain, but also a spanking good storm. The wind whipped up the lake, tossing whitecaps wildly against the rocky shore. We had to drag everything into the tent using our clothes trunk as a table and some overturned crates as chairs. We allowed Tom to eat with us, and he rattled around being as helpful as possible, trying to make himself indispensable so we'd invite him back. Thunder had been growling and groaning for some time and now it erupted with a crack like a cannon shot. Tom yelped and then looked embarrassed, not wanting to let on he was afraid. We could see lightning flash as if it were ripping right through the tent. Nevertheless, we had a slick supper of fish, canned tomatoes, canned pork and beans, potatoes, beets, tea, soda biscuits, and cookies.

The thunder seemed to split the sky directly overhead, and the accompanying lightning dazzled us. "Th-th-that was close," I said.

"What if we get hit?" Tom's voice was barely audible.

"Then we're dead ducks," Harold said.

I looked at Tom and saw how round his eyes were. I think he was afraid he might cry because he kept blinking them. "S-s-s-spit on your hands and s-s-s-sit on them," I said. Ernie and Harold looked at me as if I'd lost my mind, but I ignored them and nodded encouragingly at Tom. It wouldn't necessarily save him from the lightning because I'd just made it up, but if he believed in it, it would save him from being afraid. There was another tremendous thunderclap and streak of lightning and a loud crack as if the very gates of heaven had been broken up for kindling. "Something's been hit," Ernie said. Tom quickly spat on his hands and inched them under his bum.

The wind was blowing like fun, and we were afraid it would flatten our tent before we had got enough food stuffed into us to keep body and soul together. Tom mumbled, "Who cares?" He was sitting on one hand and shoving half a soda biscuit into his mouth with the other.

The storm finally blew itself out, and we crawled out into the rain to check for damage. An old pine tree – weakened by dozens of square woodpecker holes, each the size of a man's fist – had been uprooted by the wind not twenty feet from our tent. A huge platter of mossy earth clung to its roots, forming a fine windbreak for us. "Here's work," I said. Grandpa would want to see us busy with the crosscut saw at our earliest opportunity.

We had hoped to have a campfire and invite Ettie and her friends, but the rain squelched that idea. We didn't fancy staying in the tent all evening. We cleaned up our dishes in a bucket of water dragged up from the lake and, leaving them out in the rain for a good soak, made a dash for the cottage, inviting ourselves in.

The cottage folk sent up a cheer for us when we came in, even though we dripped rainwater all over the floor and furniture. "The male of the species, at last!" Ettie sang out. They had the gramophone playing a waltz and Ettie, her friends, Auntie Min, and Auntie Lizzie were swirling around bumping into each other and falling, weak with laughter, into the chairs. "Oh-oh!" Harold said, "I'm gettin' the heck out of here." He backed out into the kitchen. Grandpa had pushed his chair into a corner and had his pipe in his mouth, although it wasn't lit. He pretended he was dozing, but I think he was watching the antics of the women because every once in a while he chuckled. I leaned against the door frame, with my arms folded, and watched the way they moved their feet.

Bessie grabbed Tom and said, "You have to dance with me. You're the only one my size."

Tom pushed her away. "It's against my religion!" he yelled. "Get her away from me!" He crouched behind Grandpa's chair for protection while Bessie stamped her foot. Ernie grabbed her under the arms and twirled her right off the floor, with her legs sticking straight out, screaming with laughter. They'll probably fire us right back out the door, I was thinking.

The music ended and the gramophone needle rasped. Ettie lifted it, turned the crank, and started the piece over again. The music began a little high-pitched and too fast, at first, because she'd wound the thing too tightly. "Come on, Freddie," she said, "I'll take you on." I stood there like a stone, my mouth hanging. I didn't know the first thing about dancing. She took one arm, moved it out, bent it at the elbow, and put my hand up like a stop sign. She put her hand up into mine and placed my other hand on her waist.

I felt myself glowing like a sunrise. Ettie had me by the shoulder now and was trying to make me move forward. The others had flopped onto the daybed and the floor to watch the demonstration and to offer helpful suggestions. "Loosen up, Freddie," Auntie Min said. Stiff-kneed, I took a step forward, then one to the side, the way Ettie did. "Don't let him too close to that china cabinet," Auntie Lizzie warned. Ettie was pushing me back now, but I must have backed up onto the wrong foot because we tripped over each other, and I went sprawling on my back with Ettie on all fours over me.

"You are really the most impossible child," she said.

That irked me. I scrambled out from under her and helped her to her feet. "I'm-I'm-I'm-I'm." I had to stop for a second. "Not a child," I blurted.

"Of course you are," she said. "All men are."

I smarted under her insult while she pushed me this way and that, getting me to do what she wanted, tapping my boot with her toe when she wanted me to move it. Why would she say that when it's men who pay the bills, men who run the country?

Admiring my progress from the sidelines, Bessie said to Auntie Lizzie, "Freddie's catching on, isn't he?" I hadn't noticed, but I was. I was dancing. Pumping my arm up and down in time to the music, I asked Ettie, "How-how-how am I doing?"

"Not too badly," she said, "although you still smell like a fish."

I scowled down at my big feet and thought, men may be children, but at least they're not forever throwing insulting remarks around.

7

Poor Old Tom

(Harold fell in the lake today with all his clothes on.) After breakfast we boys hiked back in the bush a couple of miles. We gathered a few sacks of pine knots, got back around eleven with our load, and found the Bessie boat had come out from town bringing Grandma, Auntie Ede, and Uncle Will. After dinner we all went to the sandy bathing place for a swim, with Mr. McAlpine joining us. The water was warm and we had a fine time. While we were at the bathing place, Auntie Min, Ettie, and Mr. McAlpine wanted to row to Stonehouse Point to look for Indian arrowheads, but instead we suggested a detour up near Oliver's place, which no one objected to, and then we rowed back to the cottage and had supper.

Nothing has changed at the Oliver place. When we rowed past, it still looked untouched. Harold was disappointed, but hasn't given up scheming. He thinks we should just go in and take what we want.

I think Ettie and Auntie Min are being exceptionally polite to each other, but I get the feeling they don't mean it. The way to figure out women is, just look at the other side of the coin. If their politeness is too gushy, they are probably ready to gouge each other's eyes out. This is only a theory, as yet.

Harold wouldn't tell how he came to fall in the lake with all his clothes on, but later on Bessie let the cat out of the bag. She said, "Do you know what he was up to? Peeping at the ladies putting on their bathing costumes! He'll be the death of us, that boy! Luckily, Ettie looked out and saw him in the tree outside the window, and she tore after him with a boat paddle and chased him all the way to the locks. His choice was fall in or take a good hiding, and I must say, people going through the locks had a fablious show!"

Ernie and I had a good laugh at his expense and ribbed him, until he threatened to knock us silly.

The wind had been rising all day and by the time we Beaver Campers finished supper, there were whitecaps sweeping up the lake. We made sure our guy ropes were secure as we didn't fancy having the tent topple over in the night. Grandpa said, "You town folk had better get a hustle on if you're taking the *Bessie* boat back tonight. That wind's blowing up for a good howl."

Will said, "It'll be all right in the canal. It hardly ever gets rough in there," and Grandma muttered, "Hardly ever isn't good enough for me."

Auntie Min said, "Perhaps I should go back, too, for a few days." And Ettie said, "I thought we were to have a picnic with Mr. McAlpine?" And Auntie Min said, "I didn't know my presence was requested." And Ettie said, "I didn't realize you needed a specially engraved invitation."

Auntie Lizzie said, "Ye gods and little fishes."

The wind howled all night, and next day the lake was as rough as ever we'd seen it. The sky had partially cleared and the sun, when it broke through, made everything look clean and brilliant, the way it sometimes does after an August storm.

Right after breakfast, instead of sailing up to Rideau Ferry for provisions, we borrowed Mr. Buchanan's horse and wagon. This time we were kind enough to include Tom on the expedition, and Ernie and Harold and Tom and I stopped in at farms along the road to buy vegetables, eggs, potatoes, milk, fresh bread, and, at the Rideau Ferry store, a supply of chocolate. Tom had scribbled a postcard to Papa and asked me to buy him a stamp. The postmistress is also the store-keeper so I had a bit of a wait for the stamp. Idly, I glanced at Tom's scrawl. "Dear Papa," I read, "The cottage life agrees with us and we are all eating plenty and growing tall and strong. I am getting to be a dandy swimmer and can go like sixty. Your loving son, Tom."

He looked up and noticed me frowning down at his card. "The gos-gos-gospel truth isn't one of your strong points, is it?"

"You're not supposed to read other people's mail!" he said. He grabbed the card, licked the stamp, pounded it into place, and jabbed it through the slot in the counter.

When we got back to the locks, Mr. Buchanan was sending the steam yacht *Aileen* through the upper lock, as sleek a boat as any on the lake. She's a small excursion boat and looked to have about thirty or forty people on board. "Americans," Mr. Buchanan told us, pointing over his shoulder with his thumb. We left the horse and wagon for a moment and went up close to have a look at the Americans sitting in the cabin, looking out through the many windows along the *Aileen's* sixty-foot length. A few men were out smoking on the after-deck. "Maghty fan day," a chap called to us, and we agreed. "Windy, though," Harold said, and the man replied, "Maghty windy." Americans look pretty much like us, but seem to have a habit of speaking through their noses. "Hope the weather holds for you," Ernie said.

The windows had drop curtains that could be lowered if the weather turned bad, which it now looked as though it could do, the way the clouds were closing in. I spent a moment admiring the craftsmanship that went into building the boat as she lay waiting in the lock. Stained wood – oak, I think – sturdy, not very wide, maybe a twelve-foot beam.

Even the skiff she towed from her stern was a gem – oak

ribs, stained and gleaming like the larger craft, and not a scratch on it. I would be proud to be the captain of the *Aileen*, I thought. Besides hiring herself out for excursions to Portland and Westport, she carried provisions and mail to cottagers along the way.

We put the horse in the pasture behind the lockmaster's stable and, by the time we unloaded our own provisions and got down to the lower lock, he had locked the boat through and was waving us to come back. "Letter for you," he called.

The *Aileen* had brought it out from town at Grandma's request. Ernie ran back and fetched it from him and opened it. "It's from Papa," he said. Among other things, Papa said he was still planning to pay a visit as soon as he could comfortably leave the store. "I was going to keep it as a surprise," he wrote, "but now I believe it would be better to let you in on my plan. Your Uncle Alfred and I are thinking of jointly buying some property on the lake. He thinks it a good investment and I am inclined to agree. I understand there is plenty available if you know who to approach. Keep your ears open for any good buys."

"Does that mean we won't be able to stay with Grandpa Hicks anymore?" Tom asked.

Ernie said, "It'll be great! A place to ourselves."

"And leave me with all the women!" Harold said.

"I d-d-don't think it will ever happen."

"Why not?" They were all looking at me, puzzled.

"Papa isn't the cot-cot-cottage type."

"Of course he is," Ernie said. "Why would you say that? He's all for making us strong and healthy and making sure we build our characters right."

"Us, yes." But I could see Ernie didn't believe me.

You can't change Ernie's mind about anything, once he's got an idea in his head. He's never stopped believing in fairy tales, either. Bad-tempered kings who mend their ways, or ogres who turn out to have hearts of gold. Those are his favorites.

"You'll see," he said. "Let's hope we'll have our raft built by the time he comes. He'll take pity on us and be our first paying customer for a tour of the drowned lands."

You could almost see Tom's ears bending toward Ernie. "What raft? Whataya mean, raft?" Harold aimed a killing look at Ernie.

Ernie said, "I didn't say anything about a raft."

"Yes, you did. I heard you."

"You're hearing things, Tom. I said 'laugh.' I hope we can have a good laugh when Papa comes because he wasn't in a very good mood when we left."

"He said 'raft,' didn't he, Freddie?"

Having a secret. Building a raft. The whole idea sounded infantile, now. "It's just a raft, for Pe-Pe-Pe . . . heaven's sake. Why not let Tom in on it?"

Harold said, "Oh, sure. Why not let Ettie and Auntie Min in on it, and Bessie and Grandpa and my mother and Nora, especially Nora? We want her in on it more than anything in the world, don't we, Fred?"

"Who's Nora?" Tom asked.

"Who's Nora?" Harold smirked. "Tell him, Freddie. You want him to know all our business. Tell him how you pine for Nora; how you dream of kissing her right on the lips, Freddie."

"I do not!" I grabbed the sack of potatoes, hoisted it onto my shoulder, and headed for the cottage. Ernie, with a half-bushel basket filled with ears of corn, caught up. "Sorry I mentioned it," he said. I wanted to shrug to let him know it didn't matter, but I couldn't with a sack of potatoes on my shoulder. I elbowed him in the side of the head, and he yelled and then he grinned when he saw I wasn't mad.

Harold and Tom trudged along behind with the rest of our supplies. I could hear Tom's high voice asking, "What raft, Harold, what raft? Can I go, too? Are you letting girls on it? You shouldn't let girls on it; it'll sink." And I could hear Harold's voice saying, "There's no raft, so pipe down. Just pipe down, Tom. Tom, shut up!"

When we got back to our camp we found Ettie down on the point with Grandpa's big field glass, the wind buffeting her from behind, trying to blow her right into the drink. "What's going on?" Harold yelled.

She took the glass away from her eye and called back, "It's the *Aileen*. She's lost her rowboat; it's come loose." I put down my burden and went down to the point to have a look. I adjusted the eyepiece and soon saw the big steam yacht floundering in the huge waves crashing broadside against her as she attempted to turn back for her skiff. "Wh-wh-what's the captain thinking of?" I said. "He'll capsize." The other boys had caught up and each of us, in turn, had a look. Even without the field glass, you could make out the passenger boat rocking like mad amongst the whitecaps, listing badly, probably taking on a bit of water.

"I'd be scared stiff," Ettie said, "if I were on board. And mighty seasick, too."

"Look, he's giving up," Ernie said. We each had another look. The *Aileen* was heading up the lake again toward Rideau Ferry, and the rowboat was bobbing and dipping in the waves like a chip of wood. If it took in enough water it would sink, or if it was dashed against the shore, it would be destroyed.

"L-l-l-let's get the *Jumbo* and go rescue it," I said.

"Count me out," Ettie said. "I have no desire to risk my life for an old rowboat."

"It's not-not-not just an old rowboat," I said.

"What is it, then?"

"A-a w-w-w-work of art."

Harold snorted. "Oh, Nora," he squeaked in his ridiculous falsetto, "isn't this just the sweetest work of art? Let's not go for a row in the boat; let's hang it on the wall."

"Nora?" Ettie said. "Why Nora?"

"Haven't you heard?" Harold said.

"Give it up, Harold," I said, and headed for the boathouse to get the *Jumbo* out.

I guess even Harold has his limits. He stopped tormenting me in front of Ettie and, just as Ernie and I began to shove the boat out of the slip, he grabbed the bow and climbed in. Tom was sitting in the stern – eyes bright, scarcely breathing – hoping no one would notice him and make him stay onshore. Poor old Tom, I was thinking, how's he ever going to grow up right if we don't show him the ropes? "Grab-grab-grab the tiller, Tom," I said, "and steer us."

Ernie and I, each with a pair of oars, had to row like fun to get around the rocks sticking up along the point that sheltered the boathouse. Slate-colored clouds had knit together and hung over us like full hammocks threatening a deluge. The *Aileen* was well on her way up the lake, making good time with the wind at her back, while the skiff rocked along on the waves toward a gap in the shoreline: a shallow, stump-filled bay, part of the drowned lands. Harold offered to take a turn at the oars, but neither Ernie nor I would trade seats with him.

We had to steer in toward the little bay if we were to rescue the skiff, but each time Tom pushed against the tiller, he sent us teetering over the crest into the trough between the waves, making us rock so hard we took in water over the side. Whenever we did this, Tom lurched and clung to the tiller to keep from falling overboard.

"Get that kid off the tiller!" Harold yelled from the bow. I frowned, pretending I hadn't heard him. "Somebody else steer!"

I jerked hard on my right oar and tried to tell Tom to steer us straight up the lake again, but it wouldn't come out right. Tom had a kind of panicky look on his face and pulled the tiller toward him as hard as he could, sending us crashing over another crest. Water came pouring in over the stern, drenching Tom, making him gasp. I looked back over my shoulder and saw Harold scrambling over Ernie, and then over me, to get control of the rudder. "Get up in the bow," he yelled at Tom.

Tom stood up just as an enormous wave smacked us broadside. He pitched sideways, lost his balance, and was tossed backward into the lake. I started pulling off my boots, yanking at the laces, breaking them. Ernie was trying to grab at him from over the side of the boat, but the waves kept washing over Tom's head. Harold was swearing and pushing on my oars to move us back toward Tom. Ernie saw me pull my trousers off and then my shirt, and said, "I've just about got him. Soon as he comes up again."

I went in headfirst over the side anyway because, although he brags about his progress, Tom can't swim a stroke. He pretends he can, but he rarely takes his feet off the bottom. I watched him once, underwater.

I saw him underwater now, legs kicking out, arms thrashing. I swam under him and gave him a boost, my legs scissoring, propelling myself up, too. Our heads emerged at the same time, but he was choking so hard he couldn't get his breath. Another wave washed over him, and then another.

I tried to heave him up toward Ernie, but I didn't have enough strength, and we both went back down again. Underwater, I saw his eyes, white with panic, and I think he knew, in that instant, what his chances were. Maybe my eyes looked the same because I saw clearly what a fine line there is between survival and death. Underwater it's easier to die than to live. I grabbed at him, caught him by the hair, and pulled him up to the surface. I had him by the neck, his head in the crook of my arm like a large doll, as I swam on my side toward the boat.

Ernie and Harold were both reaching out for him. He was no longer thrashing. When I kicked hard trying to lift him up, his head lolled and his arms hung limp. Ernie and Harold caught him by the shirt and pulled his rag of a body up over the side of the boat.

If he was dead, I didn't want to live. I shouldn't have let him come in the boat in the first place. My little brother. I shouldn't have wasted time taking off my boots and my pants. I saw in my mind Mama's cold lip and cheek, gray as ice. Now Tom.

I don't know why she died. They didn't tell me till it was too late – I don't even know whether I could have saved her. But Tom, I should have been able to save Tom. I felt my strength draining away. I hadn't the power to stretch above the crest of the next wave. Choking on a mouthful of water, I went under. Instinctively, I kicked until I surfaced and heard myself rasp, trying to take in air. Ernie's head bobbed in the water near mine, and I felt myself being pushed toward the boat. I clung to the gunwale and coughed until I could breathe again. I felt Harold pulling on my arms and Ernie pushing from behind and, as my breath returned, so did my strength, enough, at least, to get me back into the boat. I helped Ernie drag himself in, weighted down as he was with all his clothes on.

Tom was lying half on the seat in the stern and half on the floorboards, his eyes closed and his nose all snotty. I couldn't see him breathing. I sat on the floorboards and hugged him as tight as I could, again and again, because I'd read that you can sometimes revive a drowned person and, in a moment, water gushed out of his mouth and nose and he started to cry. I hugged him again anyway, to make sure all the water was out of him, or maybe just because I was so glad he was alive. I wiped off his face with my shirt and wrapped it around him because he was shivering like the dickens. "Better head-head-head for home," I said.

Ernie was shivering, too, as he pulled on one pair of oars, his face so white you could see blue veins in his forehead. Harold, pale too, pulled on the other pair of oars, his lips tightly clasped. By this time, the *Jumbo* had drifted into the drowned lands, and the boys had to row in short, sharp strokes to keep us from being thrashed to bits by stumps and submerged rocks. Tom's breath still came in little sobs, but he was sitting up now in the bottom of the boat, huddled under my shirt. I sat close to him, shivering in my drawers, and he tried to spread the shirt around me, but it wouldn't stretch that far.

I peered over the side of the boat to see where we'd got to. "Look," I said, "there's the skiff." The boat we had set out to rescue was drifting in amongst the fallen trees, butted by the wind against exposed rocks. "It's gonna get wrecked," Tom croaked. "Let's go get it."

We older boys looked doubtfully at each other. I said, "We should just go-go-go home and put Tom to bed."

"Come on," Tom urged. "I'm not a baby, you know."

Where he'll be safe, I was going to say, but that's no guarantee. They said my mother died in her sleep.

I looked at him hunched in the bottom of the boat, his eyes all puffy and red, but color back in his face. When he was about three years old, a friend of my mother's brought her little lad to play, and I remember making a big thing of the other kid and ignoring Tom because he wasn't half so quaint or amusing. And I remember how Tom sat down on the bottom step and looked at me, with his eyes all droopy and sad, knowing for the first time in his life that he wasn't my favorite. Later when he was asleep, I looked in on him, and he looked so innocent lying on his back, his hands beside his head, palms up, fingers gently curled, so unprotected. I wanted to hug him and even rock him. Hardly a manly feeling, I know. Only nine and already a disgrace to Papa. So I didn't.

Tom whispered because it hurt to talk loudly, "We can't go home without the boat."

I don't know how anyone can figure out the safest course to take. Maybe he's right. We can't treat him like a baby. If we do, he'll never be anything but a baby.

"Wha-wha-what the heck," I said. I looked up at Ernie and then at Harold. They both shrugged, waiting for me to make the decision. In for a penny, in for a pound. We headed for the stumps.

Ernie and Harold shipped the oars, and then used one each to pole us into the shallows among the lily pads rippling in the wind, their blossoms upturned and tipping like stacked cups. I got up into the bow with another oar to shove us away from treacherous obstacles. Tom remained in the stern cheerfully shouting orders at us, his voice so hoarse it made him cough, proud of his new status: beloved brother, rescued from a watery grave.

The skiff had become wedged between two standing trees, which had brought it to a halt. I leaned over the bow, searching the depths for dangers, and saw an old iron cart wheel. Fallen trees lay on the bottom of what was now the lake, but was once a grove of cedars.

I motioned Harold and Ernie over to the left to avoid a buildup of stones piled up, maybe, by some long-ago farmer clearing a field. We dodged a piece of driftwood, but before we knew what had happened, we were jolted to an abrupt stop on top of the remains of a split rail fence. Ernie and Harold rocked the *Jumbo* from side to side to set us free, but we were instantly carried swiftly by the wind against the pile of rocks. We heard a sickening crunch and crack as the rudder broke off and surfaced. Tom leaned out to grab it, and Ernie grabbed Tom to prevent his falling out of the boat again. The wind dashed us against the rocks a second time before we could pole ourselves away, and I thought of my recurring dream about shoals. It's true: there are always shoals of one kind or another out there, but I'm still afloat. We all are.

We were close enough to the skiff now to grab hold of it and pull it free. It was completely intact, but badly banged up. We got what was left of the rope and tied it to our stern rope. It was a tough row home, but we took turns and, as we got closer to Sunnybank, saw Grandpa down on the point with the field glass, and Auntie Lizzie beside him, and Ettie and Auntie Min and Bessie and somebody else. And hell's bells! I could see now who it was! Nora!

"Fire my pants up here!" I yelled at Tom from the bow. Tom tried to throw them, but he was too weak. Ernie grabbed them before they blew overboard. I wriggled into them down in the bottom of the boat because I started thinking about this fellow, who lives not too far from us in Kemptville, who they lock up in the stable whenever they have company because the minute he sees the ladies, he starts tearing his clothes off for the sheer pleasure of hearing them scream. If I keep turning up in the buff in front of Nora, she'll get the impression I'm like that.

We all looked half-drowned, which some of us were, rather than merely drenched, as we angled into the boat slip, including Harold, who'd got his bath when the waves came in over the side of the boat. "Don't tell," Tom whispered. Our eyes met, all of us, and we nodded and shrugged. Nobody else needed to know how careless we'd been. Tom was growing up just fine. We were plain lucky he was going to grow up at all.

Grandpa looked old and tired when we pulled into the boathouse, bedraggled bunch that we were, and Auntie Lizzie said, "We were worried sick about you, just sick. What's wrong with Tom? He looks like a dog's breakfast."

No one said anything for a moment. "Seasick," Tom said then. We all nodded and started to describe his awful retching and vomiting, and just about made ourselves and everyone else sick as well. Except for Nora, who was looking from one to the other of us as if we had escaped from an insane asylum.

8

The Woman Question

This morning we managed to rescue the skiff belonging to the Aileen *and towed it back to Sunnybank. A friend of Ettie's was there when we arrived, but didn't stay. Just before supper, the steam yacht came back to be locked through and, as the wind had gone down a considerable degree by this time, we rowed the skiff back to her. The captain was very grateful and said he hoped we hadn't put ourselves in any danger. We said we hadn't and he thanked us.*

The reason Nora was there when we got back from rescuing the skiff was because she was delivering invitations to the dance they were having at the Coutts House at Rideau Ferry. Ettie wanted her to stay, but she wasn't able. "Couldn't you come back tomorrow?" Ettie asked. "We'd love to have you come for supper, wouldn't we, Mother?"

"We would indeed," Auntie Lizzie said, but then what else could she say? She added that we camp boys could join in to make it more festive, and Ettie gave her a killing look.

The next day was fine and clear and I can remember feeling excited all day waiting for Nora to arrive, although I can't recall one thing we had for supper that night. Oh, wait, I know. Corn on the cob. And Ettie complained and said, "The boys are eating like pigs again, Mother." And Auntie Lizzie said, "No one is required to look at them." And everyone laughed except me because I didn't want to be considered a mere boy, much less, a pig. I put my chewed-off cob on my plate and refused another, even though I'd had only seven and I'm trying to beat Ernie's record of eleven. Now that I think about it, we also had small potatoes boiled in their jackets and fried fish caught by Ernie, Harold, and me, and apple fritters. Quite a feast, all in all.

As usual there was plenty of chitchat around the table. Auntie Min quizzed up Nora, asking her a lot of questions about her family and the friends staying with them at Rideau Ferry. "One of our friends is very old," Nora replied to Min, "in his nineties, and is like a great-uncle to us. We're very fond of him." She said, "He has a remarkably strong constitution, although sometimes we feel his mind is slipping. We think he has bad dreams and can't get out of them, even after he's wide awake. Sometimes he shakes his head slowly from side to side, the tears just pouring down. There's nothing we can do for him when he's like that. It's sad."

"It's a terrible affliction to be old," Grandpa said to the company in general. "I mind the times I used to go tearing about scandalizing the older generation, and now what do I do? Sit and doze. Sit and doze and put myself at the mercy of the younger generation."

"Waited on hand and foot by your daughters, you might add," Auntie Lizzie said, pouring out more tea for him. "And issuing orders like the lord high admiral. Oh yes, you're badly treated indeed."

"Well, well, I know I'm a burden, but it won't be long before they'll be measuring me for the old pine box."

"Somebody strike up the violins," Auntie Lizzie said.

Auntie Min said, "Now, now, Father. Lizzie doesn't mean to be cranky."

Auntie Lizzie said, "Yes I do."

Cousin Ettie said, "Can we not have one moment of intelligent conversation at this table?" Everyone was silent.

"Apparently not," said Auntie Lizzie.

After an awkward moment or two, the general buzz started again and I felt safe striking up a conversation with Nora, who was sitting almost across from me beside Ettie. I wanted to bring the conversation around to the dance that was to take place soon. I pretty well had to shout to make sure she'd hear me over the din of Ernie asking for more corn, and Auntie Lizzie telling him he had a hollow leg, and Bessie complaining that Tom was taking all the room with his elbows on the table. Loudly I began, "Are-are-are-" and had to stop. Blinking hard I managed, "You-you-you." Suddenly, for who knows what reason, everyone was quiet. "A-a-a." I heard myself shrieking. "Good dan-dan-dan dancer?" I got my voice down to a whisper.

"Pardon?" she said.

Oh, Lord. It's hard enough to say things once. I sat there like a dummy, my mouth dry, knowing my Adam's apple was bobbing up and down as if I had a tennis ball in there I was hoping to swallow. All around the table eyes turned to me, then to Nora, then back to me. "He wants to know if you'll dance with him," Bessie piped up, and my eyes nearly bulged out of my head with embarrassment. Across from me, Ettie was brushing at her cheek in a meaningful way and staring at my face with a frown and nodding, until I got the idea and brushed my hand across my own cheek. I had pieces of corn smeared across my face from ear to ear, apparently.

"Why, I'd be happy to dance with you," Nora said. I thought she looked a little bit astonished to be asked. She smiled, shyly at first, looking down at her hands in her lap. But then her eyes met mine and she smiled. At first you would think it a mischievous, impish smile, but then you realize how warm and sincere it is. It's the sweetest smile I have ever seen. It made me soar right up out of my embarrassment. I knew at that moment that someday she would love me.

She was smiling, now, at the other young people, saying

she hoped they'd be able to come to the dance at Rideau Ferry, and they were all nodding and smiling back except Tom. "I'm never dancing," he said.

"Not even if I ask you and say, 'Pretty-please-with-cream-and-sugar-on-it?'"

Tom tried to scowl and look away, but even he seemed to fall victim to Nora's flashing eyes and playful grin. "I dunno," he said, with the corners of his mouth going up, "maybe." And then he turned pink and put his napkin up over his face and made everyone laugh.

While the ladies did the supper dishes, we campers got a rattling good bonfire going and rolled another log alongside to provide plenty of seating. By the time the ladies arrived, accompanied by Grandpa, we had a fine show prepared for them with Harold playing the concertina, Ernie the drum, and me the mouth organ. We played "Darling Nellie Gray," "Camptown Races," "Abide With Me," and then, because we ran out of tunes we all knew, "God Save the King," and everybody got up and stood at attention. They clapped at the end of our concert, and Auntie Lizzie called, "Encore!" We had to decline and admit that we'd run through our entire repertoire.

"Then Fred will just have to sing for us," she said.

"Too-too-too hoarse," I said.

Auntie Min and Ettie started in then and yelled, "We vote for Fred; three cheers for Fred," and Ettie pulled on my arms until I stood up. Usually I don't mind singing because it's the only thing I can count on doing pretty well, but I felt shy in front of Nora. I remembered what she had said about some man she knows who stutters except when he makes a speech, and I wondered if I could imagine myself singing whenever I had to talk to anyone.

I sang "Beautiful Dreamer" and the words came out as clear and sharp and smooth as if I'd painted them in the air with my voice as a brush. "Beautiful dreamer, wake unto me," I sang. "Starlight and dewdrops are waiting for thee." I kept singing the words, looking up toward the trees, not looking at any one person, until I got to the line, "Beautiful dreamer, queen of my song." I couldn't help it; I had to look right at Nora and saw her sitting on the log beside Ettie, leaning toward me, her elbows on her knees and her chin propped on her knuckles, with her lips turned up just a little bit because she was perfectly happy and her eyes, wide and serious, shining for me and me alone. When I finished, everyone was quiet for a moment and I was afraid they all thought there was another verse, but I didn't know any more. Then they all clapped, and Auntie Lizzie wiped her eyes on her apron and said it was the most heartfelt rendition she had ever heard. Grandpa coughed and blew his nose and said, "Didn't somebody mention popcorn and taffy?"

When it was time to walk up to the lockmaster's barn to hitch up Nora's horse and see her into her buggy and on the road back to Rideau Ferry, I walked beside her and asked if she wasn't a little frightened to drive alone at night. "Not in the least," she said. "Should I be?"

"The ferryman might get you," Ernie said, "or his ghost."

"Who's that?" she asked. "What do you mean?"

Ernie looked embarrassed, then, because he remembered (a little late) that the villainous ferryman was related somehow to the white-haired gentleman, the close friend of her family. Harold didn't remember a thing. "They say he was the wickedest man alive and if his ghost catches you late at night, it'll stab you with an icepick and drink all your bl . . . ow!" I had just managed to stab him with the point of my elbow.

"Make them stop, Mother," Ettie said.

Auntie Lizzie said, "That's enough, boys; you'll have Nora's hair standing right on end. You can stay the night with us, dear, if you think your folks won't worry." Nora was still staring quizzically at Harold, obviously not aware of her elderly friend's evil relative.

"Why not stay over?" Ettie repeated.

"Oh, I couldn't. My mother would kill me. I'd rather meet a hundred ghosts than listen to her tell me how cruel I am, and how I never think of anyone but myself." In a mocking voice she said, " 'You're so thoughtless and so careless and you can't see one step beyond yourself.' Anyway, I don't believe in ghosts. I defy anyone's ghost to haunt me."

She took my hand and shook it and said, "I loved your singing. I wouldn't be surprised if you made a career of it. I hope you'll invite me to your first public concert."

After she'd gone and we were walking back to the cottage from the road where we'd waved good-bye, Ettie said, "Nora aims to be one of the 'new' women and I think she's making a pretty fair start."

"What-what-what does that mean?"

"An intellectual. She says women ought to be able to vote and wear men's clothes whenever they want."

"Why-why-why would they want to? They'd look ugly, all woo-woo-woolly and tweedy."

She added, "And smoke in public."

"A pipe?"

"Cigarettes, I think."

I stayed awake late that night, writing in my head the song I would sing to Nora at my first public concert. Some of the lines praised her starry eyes and her kissable lips, and some of the lines described the way my legs feel weak when I stand close to her, and some of the lines asked her to marry me in a couple of years as soon as I'm old enough. By then I will have outgrown my speaking problem and I'd say, *See here, Nora, I think you look more beautiful in a dress than a pair of britches.* And she'd say, *Oh, Frederick, I want to stay beautiful for you always and I would never dream of taking up tobacco.*

And then I started thinking that I would definitely have to have a job and a good one, too, if I intended to support a wife. Maybe a job in the city was a good idea. It would be bound to pay better than any job I might get involving boats, or charting courses through unknown waterways. What a lot of responsibility I was letting myself in for, I thought. Having a job and being married would take up my whole life, and there wouldn't be much time left over for larking about with the other boys.

But then I'd have Nora by my side. That's the good part. Still . . . I must have been starting to fall asleep because I don't know why else I felt sad. I was thinking, nothing will ever be the same.

9

I'll Grind His Bones to Make My Bread

Ettie's friend stayed for supper last night. After supper we boys felt generous and invited everyone to a bonfire on the point near our tent. We put on a concert and had popcorn, and Auntie Min made a lot of syrup out of brown sugar and poured it over the corn. It was delicious. This mixture is what the Yankees call Cracker Jack. We had a swell time eating it. This morning before breakfast, Harold and Ernie and I went back to the bush and got twisted walking sticks. Then Grandpa announced he had a goodly number of chores for us.

Grandpa said, "I think if you look, you'll find the crosscut saw hanging in the icehouse."

Ernie and I can work pretty well together on the saw because we're about the same size. We managed to get a rhythm going, one on either side of the tree that had fallen during the storm the other day, pulling back and forth on the saw until our elbows gave out. Harold hacked the branches off the old pine with the axe, and then we all took turns splitting the wood for the cottage stove, keeping back some of the bigger pieces for our campfire. By the time we'd hauled the wood up behind the cottage and stacked it to Grandpa's satisfaction, it was dinnertime.

"Why don't you take it easy for a change this afternoon?" Grandpa said to us. "A nice row in the *Jumbo* is just what you lads need." He gave us a wink and a half-dollar each. We didn't need a second invitation. After dinner we rowed past the shack at Oliver's landing to see if any workmen had arrived, but the place was deserted; not a single log or board had been removed. "Let's pull the boat up onshore and have a look around," Harold suggested. "We could easily break into the place."

"You go, we'll pick you up later," Ernie said.

"Sissy!" Harold said.

Ernie started looking as though he might go after all. To him, sissy is the worst word in the English language, and I guess I'm not too fond of it myself. Anyway, if he went, I'd be the only one left sitting like a priss in the boat. I said, "Ernie and I don't have to tres-tres-tres invade someone's prop-prop-prop cabin to prove our bravery."

"Spoken like a true coward," Harold said.

I have to admit, I agreed with him. I sounded like a sap. But if I'd tried to explain how I really felt, it would have taken about a day and a half. I couldn't get the old man out of my mind, remembering how tormented he'd sounded when he was begging not to have the cabin sold or torn down. Who was he, I wondered, and why did he rant on so much about not tearing the cabin down? And I thought about what Nora had said about his mind going. I wouldn't want to make him worse. What if we caused him to lose his mind completely? What if it killed him?

We drifted along the shore eyeing the place. It was one of those soft days we get now and again when the only energy you can muster goes into daydreaming, and you have a feeling in the back of your mind that what you wish for will come true. The breeze came in puffs like someone out of breath, panting with excitement so that it rippled the lake, here and there, into lips turned up for kisses. I would write something like that in my journal, except for the fact that someone might read it.

We'd stripped off our shirts to row in our undervests, the better to feel the sun beating down, frying our bare shoulders. I was leaning over the bow of the boat, my chin on one arm, trailing my hand in the water. Harold and Ernie were not day-dreaming. They were sizing up Oliver's shack, what we could see of it through the trees.

"I bet they wouldn't mind giving us a couple of those logs."

"We'd need more than a couple. They're not that big around."

"How would we get them home?"

"Tow them, of course."

"We should ask for some floor planks, too, if they're not too rotten."

"Come on, let's pull the boat up and poke around," Harold said.

I said, "Na, t-t-too hot."

"I always knew you were chickenhearted."

"I'm n-n-n-not."

"It's pretty hot, all right," Ernie said. "I think I'm getting sunstroke."

"Cluck-cluck-cluck," Harold said.

"There's nothing to see," I said. "Why-why-why don't we just wait for the workmen to come tear it down?"

"What are you scared of? The bogeyman might getcha?"

"Don't be a hor-hor-hor-horse's ass, Harold. I'm not scared of anything." But I was. Not of any one thing, just generally jittery. If the cabin was full of snakes, I'd be upset, but not scared; or porcupines, I'd back away smartly; or skunks, well, I don't even want to think about the result of that. Those are things I could deal with. But the old man never really explained why he didn't want the place torn down. That's what was bothering me most. He had said it was evil and that there was a curse on it, said it with such horror in his voice that it had made my skin crawl.

I have a feeling Ernie believes in curses. I'd like to say I don't, but maybe I do, too. I wish I could say to Ernie, *Look, I'm your older brother, I'll protect you.* That's a laugh! I'm cursed with nerves that are so bad I wouldn't be able to protect a housefly.

I thought about old Oliver and his wife, and shuddered. If Grandpa's story was true, they got their fun from catching people and slitting them open like so many fish bellies. It couldn't be true. A chill ran up and down the length of my spine. Why would anyone do that? Not even animals kill without a purpose. I shivered again and felt queasy.

The *Jumbo* nosed against a fallen tree jutting into the water. "I'm-I'm-I'm staying in the boat," I said. Harold reached out for a branch, pulled us in to shore, and hopped past me out over the bow. He tied the rope to a tree branch. "Let's go, Ernie," he said. "We'll leave little Freddie-girl here to tend his knittin'."

Ernie had turned around to face the bow, but was still sitting in the oar seat with his elbows on his knees. He glanced quickly at me from under his eyebrows, and looked away. I could tell he was up against a dilemma. On the one hand he hated to be called a sissy, but on the other hand, we were usually loyal to each other. We stuck up for each other most of the time. To be loyal, he'd have to stay behind with me and have Harold jeer at him for the next eighty years of his life.

Or I could give him a break.

"Let's-let's-let's get this over with," I sighed.

The small log structure stood not far from the water, on a rise. Nearby, we could make out the remains of a larger building, burned, likely; its crumbled, charred foundation all but obliterated by an overgrowth of mullein and milkweed and wild raspberry.

The surviving cabin crouched amidst the dense bush and low scrub. A bank of sumacs fanned the front of the place, raising blood-colored spears against intruders. Pines, grown tall behind it, cast it in gloom even in the afternoon sunlight. Junipers grew thick and high right up to the barred door, as if nature wanted to pretend the building wasn't there. It leaned slightly, probably pushed by the prevailing winds, its walls weathered black.

The roof looked on the point of collapse under a buildup of moldy-green moss. I thought, if we so much as push on the door, it'll fall on our heads. The door was not only criss-crossed with boards nailing it shut, but padlocked. The window was boarded up as well. It was hard to get close to the place because of the prickly juniper bushes. Ernie said, "We should have brought our walking sticks with us."

Juniper grows like a natural trap. If you try not to care whether you get pricked by its needles and just wade into it, it trips you up in its intermeshing branches, which lie close to the ground. A series of ouches came from us as we tried to push our way between bushes, some of them waist-high. We should have had our shirts on for better protection, but we'd left them in the boat.

Harold led us around to the back of the place to see if there was any way in. Thick tangles of wild raspberry clung to us and scratched our arms and chests. There was another window at the back, also boarded up. I saw an old cast-iron cauldron in amongst the trees, leaning against a stump, with a round bottom like those used to boil down maple sap to get syrup. Not many maple trees, though, not enough to tap. I had a picture in my mind of the ferryman's wife stewing up her disgusting mess.

"Okay, it's a lost-lost-lost cause. Let's go."

Harold looked disappointed, but was scheming still about how to break in. Ernie looked relieved, and I wasn't looking where I was going. My foot became caught in the grip of a juniper bush, and I went down hard. I felt ridiculous. I couldn't crawl forward or wriggle back until I freed my boot. There I was, propped on my outstretched arms to protect my hide from a bed of prickles, kicking for all I was worth, not able to get up and not wanting to lie down, my face inches from old Oliver's beastly shack. That's when I saw it. Something white. Yellowish-white. Bone-white. I thought it moved, wiggled like a worm, but I looked hard at it and it didn't.

Either the stone foundation had sunk into the earth, or the

earth had built itself up high around it, but the bottom log
had rotted away a little. The thing lying near the rotted log
looked like a finger bone. But that was crazy; it was a stick,
of course. A peeled stick.

I kept thinking about the stories we'd heard. What if they
were true? Some poor half-murdered person could have tried
to claw his way out of a shallow grave . . . but, no, it had to
be a stick. I twisted into a sitting position, grasped my ankle,
and yanked my foot loose. It was all rock around here,
anyway. Not enough earth to bury a fish head.

Ernie was asking if I was all right, and Harold was calling
under his breath, "Listen! Someone's coming, I think." We
heard the thud of boots, a rock kicked out of the way, the
swish-whack of a stick hitting underbrush, and the three of
us took off like flushed groundhogs scurrying for the safety
of our hole.

Once in the boat I sat in the bow and picked juniper
needles out of my belly while Ernie rowed and Harold steered.
"Don't let's go out too far," Harold said in a low voice. "We
want to see who's prowling around the place." We let ourselves drift along the shoreline a short way. Ernie whispered,
"We should have brought our fishing poles." After a minute
he removed the oars and dipped them in the water to keep the
oarlocks from squeaking. Turning, we rowed nonchalantly
back, as if we were out for our daily exercise.

We saw two men come around the corner of the shack,
wading through the juniper, both familiar to us. They wore

stout breeches and tall boots. Wilf stopped to push a walking stick against the chink between the logs, and a piece fell out. "You'll have it down in half a day," he called.

The other man, the one we'd seen sitting with the old man in the bleachers at Newboro, was trying to pry off the boards over the window. We heard him call back, "Your grandfather'll be mighty put out about it."

"He'll never find out."

"Might. I'm having second thoughts about this. Too bad to upset him, you know? Yet there's no point buying only the back half. No point buying any of it if I can't do what I want. Property up the lake I could get would do me just about as well."

"I thought we had a gentleman's agreement on this," Wilf called. He was moving back around the corner of the shack.

"I'm not too sure now. The idea of this place coming down put the old fella into an awful dither. What's it to him anyway?"

Wilf appeared again. "I don't know," he called. "He's old. Takes notions into his head that sound like nightmares. Listen, I can get the key for that padlock if you want to go in."

We let our boat drift in on the other side of the fallen tree, where we were pretty sure we were out of sight.

"No, don't bother. I've no interest in the cabin except curiosity. It's the land around it I want." He shaded his eyes with his hand and looked back at Wilf. "Say, though, I'm curious to know how your granddad was related to old John Oliver?"

"He doesn't like to talk about it. He tells people only that he ran away from home as a boy and took the name Adams to signify the start of a new life. He's lived in Ottawa so long he's all but forgotten his early life and his brute of a father."

"His father being Oliver," we heard the other man say. "Never knew he had more than one son."

"Keep it to yourself, will you? He thinks his past is cursed."

Harold let a low whistle escape at this news, and Ernie and I both punched him to shut him up. Peering out from the fallen tree's blind of branches, we saw the man turn his back on the cabin and look out over our heads across the lake. We didn't dare venture out into view at this stage. We heard the man say, "Well, I'll have to let you know whether I really want this place or not."

"My grandfather would consider lowering the price."

"Would he? I don't think he wants to sell it half as much as you do. I keep my ear to the ground. They say you're pretty fond of betting on the horses over there in the States and that you're pretty deep in debt."

"And what if I am? No skin off your nose, is it?"

"Don't suppose it is."

After a moment Wilf said, "He'll take a hundred dollars less. What do you say?" Their voices drifted away as they headed back around the log cabin in the direction of the road.

We looked skeptically at each other. The raft dream was sinking out of sight. Harold said, "Think he'll buy it anyway?"

"No," I said.

"No," Ernie said.

Harold pounded his fist on the gunwale. "Well, somebody will buy it. I'm not giving up that easily. But say, isn't that a corker about the old gent being Oliver's son? Wait till we tell them at home!"

"Harold," I said, "we-we-we aren't telling them at home."

"Why not?"

I couldn't say, exactly. Something about Nora, I think. I didn't want any shadows cast by her friends to fall across her beautiful nature. Ernie said, "They'll want to know how we came across that piece of information and then what will you say? Oh, we were just breaking into the place to steal some lumber and then we hung about spying? I guarantee Grandpa would not be pleased."

I was beginning to think beyond Nora now. "Th-th-the old man," I began.

"What about him?"

I wanted to say, *He needs his alias. It's his protection. It shields him from the curse of who he really is*, but all I could manage was, "He-he-he needs his dis-dis-disguise." I left it at that.

10

Freddie the Failure

We were up early and had breakfast and, after
breakfast, Uncle Will came down in the Bessie
and I spent some time pestering him to let me
take a turn at driving it. He said, "Later when
the time is ripe." We boys picked wild apples,
and then walked back into the woods and got a
lot of birch bark for notepaper because there
wasn't enough for a canoe. We came home and
had dinner and then took Bessie and Auntie Min
and Auntie Lizzie out for a sail in the Jumbo,
away out on the lake where it was rough, and we
had the ladies scared silly. Ettie wouldn't come
as she is feeling deserted by Mr. McAlpine, who
has decided to take up residence in the United
States. We nearly split laughing to see the ladies

turn white as ghosts. Harold and Ernie and I are expert sailors now. After we came home we read funny papers in the grove, where it is nice and cool, until supper time. We very much like the antics of that rascal Buster Brown.

After supper it was dead calm, and Uncle Will said, "Come on, Fred. The time is ripe."

"What for?" Harold wanted to know. Uncle Will wouldn't tell him, but as soon as he and Ernie saw us heading for the *Bessie*, they started clamoring to have a lesson, too.

"Later," Uncle Will said. "When the time is ripe."

I undid the ropes and we climbed down into the boat, where it was tied to the dock. It was getting on toward the end of August so the water was pretty low. Uncle Will showed me how to prime the engine by pouring gasoline into a small brass cup. Then I had to pull a lever to advance the spark and, finally, after giving the flywheel a few smart turns, got the engine going on the third try.

Uncle Will pushed us away from the dock. We put-putted slowly out into the lake, and he said, "All right, full throttle ahead!" And soon we were whistling along as slick as you please. I felt the breeze in my hair and knew a smile a yard wide was plastered all over my face.

Frederick the Navigator! I could drive boats forever. Hard to imagine, I thought, someone hiring you and paying you to do something as pleasureful as driving a boat. We went up the shore as far as Rideau Ferry, and Uncle Will said, "Let's see how good your landing skills are." I made a wide circle, cut the engine to half-throttle, and nosed in toward the dock at the Ferry. No one was around except a boy and a man fishing from the bridge, so I had nothing to distract me from concentrating hard on coming in at the best angle, slowing down, inching along, slowing, changing the angle to bring us alongside.

"Watch!" Uncle Will yelled. We were getting too close to the bridge piling so I tried going in reverse, which put my steering off. Above us on the bridge the people fishing were jerking their poles out of the way and trying to reel in their lines, so I cut the engine just as we were about to crash into the bridge abutment. Uncle Will reached out with a paddle, pushed us off, and paddled us back into safer water. I guess I looked a little rattled because he said, "Nobody gets it right the first time. Try again."

I went through the whole rigamarole of starting up the engine again and circling back. This time I kept an eye on where I was going. I selected a point on the dock where I wanted to land and headed slowly for a spot ten feet wide of it. When I brought us alongside the dock, we were bang on. In more ways than one. "Slow down! Slow down!" Uncle Will yelled. I managed to bang up the bow before Uncle Will could stave us off. He leaned over the front to check for damage. "Nothing much that a little paint won't fix," he said. "Try it again."

By now I was sweating. I brushed my arm across my upper lip and forehead, took a deep breath, and started the engine going again. I made a tighter circle this time, came in dead slow at a closer angle and, by golly, it was a perfect landing. I cut the engine. Uncle Will congratulated me, and the boy fishing from the bridge pumped his arm up and down to show, I guess, he was rooting for me.

"Try it again," Uncle Will said, "just to make sure it wasn't a fluke."

Inwardly I groaned. I was thinking, quit while you're ahead, buster. But I started up the engine, turned the wheel, and came within a whisker of whacking the stern against the dock. Uncle Will was looking a little pale, I thought. I chanced a look at the hotel lawn. Where formerly it had been almost completely uninhabited, it was now swarming with people, one of them, Nora Maberly.

Uncle Will was yelling at me, "Eyes in the back of your head!" I nodded. I made another mediocre landing and then two perfect ones in a row, not daring to check whether Nora was watching. I could tell by the look on Uncle Will's face that he was pleased with me. "Let's tie up for five minutes," he said. He waved at a couple of chaps he knew strolling along the waterfront with a girl. He tied the boat and, when I got out, he handed me a half-dollar. He leaned his head close to mine and said, "There's a pretty girl behind you, can't take her eyes off you. If you were to offer her a soda, I doubt she'd say no." I waited a full three seconds before I turned to look.

Nora stood on the grass at the edge of the dock, her unruly hair escaping its loose ribbon, her hands clasped primly behind her. She had that pixie smile I found irresistible, like a little girl about to misbehave. She said, "I wish I could operate a boat."

"N-n-n-nothing to it," I grinned. Behind her, the sun blushed through the trees as it crept slowly to bed, lending her a rosy glow. She was smiling at me and I felt myself glowing, too, and stood there smiling back. I wanted to offer to buy her a cooling drink at the store and, after several tries, I did. She said nothing would give her greater pleasure. I wish I could just open my mouth and say things like that. We walked across the uneven lawn to the road, and she slipped her arm through mine to keep from wobbling. I looked at her delicate arm lying lightly across mine, across the black hairs on my bony wrist. I wanted to caress it, but I didn't.

In the store, I simply pointed to the sodas in a pan of chipped ice, held up two fingers, slapped my money down, and the transaction went off as smooth as you please. We sat on a bench outside the store, squinting into the sunset, sipping our drinks through straws. Sitting close like this was every bit as exciting as it had been on the excursion boat. I leaned closer until our shoulders touched. She turned roguish eyes to mine and grinned as if we shared a secret joke. "Remember the peanuts?" she said. I nodded.

There was something about those eyes; they were telling me something. She likes me, I thought. She really likes me. I reached across and gently took her hand. She looked down, touched, I think, her lashes dark against her cheek. In a moment her eyes met mine, wide, innocent.

The next instant, the mischief was back. "Naughty!" she said, and pulled away, laughing. I could tell she wasn't cross, though, because her eyes never left mine.

"Nora!" we heard then. "Come along, Nora!" Someone – a girl – was calling her from the hotel veranda. "Our guests are here!"

Nora stood up. "Oh! Sorry! I've got to go, but thank you for the drink. Awfully nice to see you again." The pixie grin, a wave, and she was gone. It was as if she had never been there. I stared at my hand, hardly believing it had touched hers, had held it, and I felt feverish, as if I were coming down with something.

I made my way back down to the *Bessie* boat and I'm not sure that my feet even touched the ground. Uncle Will was sitting in it, waiting for me. "'Bout time, Romeo!" I scarcely heard him. He shook his head. "I don't think you're in fit shape to drive home."

"I am s-s-so," I said. I started the engine and we headed for home, Will chuckling about something; I don't know what.

The sun was below the trees, tinting clouds above the north shore every shade of pink and purple known to man. I kept glancing at it over my left shoulder as we sliced along through the water, and felt kind of pink and purple and radiant myself. Visions of Nora covered the inside of my mind like wallpaper. I let a sigh escape. Uncle Will was staring at me with an amused look. I said, "There's nothing like a boat." He nodded, still smiling.

Soon Sunnybank was in sight. As we got closer, I could see the folks on the dock: Bessie fishing, Tom beside her, likely telling her she wasn't holding the pole right; Harold and Ernie in their swimming togs pushing each other off the dock; Grandpa lowering the flag because it was sunset. Cousin Ettie was saluting the flag, her hair fuzzed out around her head like a halo. Auntie Min, straight backed and tidy, sat on the bench beside her sister, Auntie Lizzie, who looked dreamy and relaxed with her head back against the flagpole. They were all enjoying the scarcity of mosquitoes, who take their vacations elsewhere in this part of August. Looked like Grandma had come out from town and brought someone with her. Looked like Papa. In fact, it was Papa. He was pacing back and forth, swatting the air with his hands. Not all mosquitoes take vacations in late August.

"You're for it now, sonny-boy," Uncle Will called to me. "Bring her in for a perfect landing."

My heart started pumping overtime, and I could feel sweat running down my sides inside my shirt. An audience. I steered in fairly close to shore, which made the boys scramble to get out of the water. If I ever sang in a concert, this is what it would be like: faces turned my way, eyes focused on every twitch and tremble of my muscles, minds making themselves up about whether or not I was any good. I took a big breath, and another, and another, and went putting right on past Sunnybank.

I went way down past Mr. Ash's, our neighbor to the east, and had to steer out from shore pretty sharply because there were submerged shoals down this way. I kept looking down into the water, but I was well away from them.

"Come on, laddie, it's do or die!" Uncle Will was getting impatient. I wheeled to the right, came around in a wide sweep, gritted my teeth hard, and headed back toward Sunnybank. I blocked out every single person on the dock, saw only the angle the boat made with the shore, eased her in and around, slowed, reversed ever so slightly, brought her smartly alongside, and cut the engine.

Cheers went up. I sat there not wanting to look at anyone, not even Papa. I rubbed water drops off the gunwales with my shirtsleeves. Uncle Will put out the bumpers and threw the bow rope up as he hoisted himself out. I looked up then and watched him go over and shake hands with Papa. Papa said something about having business in the area, that he'd come to stay for a few days. Then I climbed out. Papa came over to me and started congratulating me and slapped me on the back. He really slaps hard. I don't think I'll do that when I have boys. You could take it the wrong way. Grandma was trying to give me a hug, and Tom was pulling at me begging me to take him out in the boat, when Bessie started screaming her lungs out, "I caught one! I caught one!"

And had she ever! A big bass, the great-granddaddy of all bass. It took her line and would have yanked her in after it if I hadn't grabbed her. She wouldn't give up the fishing rod to my superior fish-landing abilities, so I had to help her hold the rod and show her how to ease the fellow in: ease it and hold tight, ease and hold. Tom ran down to the boathouse for the landing net and a pail, and Ettie ran up to the cottage for her camera. Once we'd got the bass safely out of the water onto the dock, Bessie leaned over it, frowning. "I thought it would be bigger," she said.

"Looks about five or six pounds. Not-not-not a bad catch for your first fish," I said.

"I'm not talking about how fat it is," she said. "I thought it would be taller. About as tall as me."

"Hold it up," Ettie said, opening out her camera, moving sideways to make the most of the fading light, staring down to find the image. "This will go down in history." It took all of Bessie's strength to stand there holding up her fish, waiting for Ettie to take her picture.

"Merciful heavens!" Grandma said. "Isn't that the *Bessie* boat floating away down the lake?"

Uncle Will said, "Oh, for the love of Mike!" He looked at me. "I thought you were tying up." But I had thought he was, as he always takes charge in that particular boat, and so I kept on standing there, with my face hanging out like a dope, instead of throwing myself into the lake to swim after the boat.

"Pair o' ninnies, the two of you," Grandpa said.

Uncle Will was already on his way to the boathouse to fetch the *Jumbo*, with Tom in hot pursuit, and still I stood there thinking, I can't win for losing. My Nora dream had long ago fizzled and disappeared. It was as though a magnet drew my eyes in Papa's direction. He stood with his arms folded, his head on a tilt, nostrils flared as though he was having trouble getting enough air into his chest. His eyes were level at half-mast, not showing anger. Showing disgust.

Grandpa had folded the Union Jack and was carrying it up to the cottage. I expect he was put out with his son, too, but it didn't seem to be spoiling his day, or Will's either, for that matter. Ettie was taking her camera back up for safekeeping. Grandma was saying to Ernie and Harold, "Off you go and get dressed, you boys, before you catch your death. Lips blue as mold on you. Goodness. And I'll make a cup of hot ginger for you," she called after them.

Papa turned away from me toward Bessie and said, "Well, now, Bessie-girl, aren't you the clever little fisherwoman. What will you do with your catch?"

"Stab it," she said, "and pull out its guts."

"Bessie! Tut-tut! I think we'd better just hand it over to one of the boys to clean. You wouldn't want your pretty hands to smell of fish."

"I don't mind."

"Well, you're a funny girl!"

"Freddie will help me."

"Yes, I'm sure he would, but all the same, I think we'll ask Ernie."

Bessie, by now, was scowling down at her fish in a pail on the dock. She let her eyes slide up to look at me as if she was trying to tell me something without speaking, but I turned to go along the stony shore to our tent.

"Frederick!" It was my father calling me. The thought ran through my mind, don't stop. What would he do? Run after me? Throw something? Hit me with his fist?

I've never seen my father run. He often hurries, but never breaks into a wild, arms flailing, knees pumping, breath gasping, actual run. And he'd never hit anyone. It's barbaric to strike others, he says. But maybe it would be good for us both to be tossed together into a boxing ring. I could just see it: neither of us knowing the first thing about throwing punches, but swinging at each other all the same. To tell the truth, I wouldn't mind giving him a good clout. Maybe he feels the same way about me.

I stopped and turned. I could see Auntie Lizzie and Auntie Min carrying the pail with Bessie's fish in it between them, heading for the boathouse, and Bessie walking ahead of them, backward, so she could keep talking to them, telling about how she would catch an even bigger one tomorrow.

Papa had his hands on his hips waiting, I guess, for me to come back. He was still on the dock. There was quite a distance between us. Out on the lake the *Bessie* boat towing the

Jumbo was putting along, with Tom steering and Uncle Will sitting beside him, giving orders.

"I'd like a word with you," Papa said.

I stood where I was on the stony shore.

"Well, I'm not going to shout!" he shouted. "Have you lost all semblance of good manners? Come when you're called."

My skin pricked and itched and tingled as if it were no longer part of me, but something mechanical dragging me along with it toward my father. I was looking at him and not at where I was going, and went over on my ankle like a girl in high-heeled slippers. He winced and looked away as I caught my balance.

He motioned for me to sit beside him on the flagpole bench, his walking stick across his knees. When we were seated he said, "Your grandfather tells me you are coming along nicely. He says that you behave well and are helpful." I bent over and pulled out a long piece of grass from a tuft growing like hay. "This is encouraging," he said. I chewed on the wisp of grass. "Don't do that, Frederick."

After a pause he said, "Well, my boy, I think it's time we had a serious talk about your future, don't you? Have you given any thought yourself to what you might do with your life?"

"N-n-n-no," I lied. I didn't want him to know how I felt about Nora, nor how I felt about boats. The two things kind of went together in my mind.

"I thought not. So, as usual, I've been obliged to do your thinking for you. I see little point in keeping you in school for much longer. One more year at most. I think you know that I had fond hopes, at one time, of seeing you in one of the professions – the law, perhaps, or the church – but your persistent inability to conduct yourself in an intelligent and mature fashion somewhat rules this out. Do you not agree?"

Did-I-not-agree? I did not. I didn't want to be a lawyer or a preacher, but that wasn't the point. The point was, he seemed to think he could read me like a book. Page three: Freddie blunders. Page seven: Freddie blunders again. His book is all about Freddie the nincompoop, who can't do anything right. But that's not the whole story. He can't seem to read between the lines. He's got one picture of me in his mind and it's entitled, Frederick the Failure.

Papa went on, not waiting for me to stumble around either agreeing or disagreeing, "You will remember that I wrote to an acquaintance of mine in Toronto. Well, I have had a reply." I felt the bottom drop out of my life and sat, empty, my head down, waiting for him to go on. "He is willing to take you into his business in a year's time."

Not this summer, at any rate, I thought, with something like relief.

"You will, of course, start at the bottom and work your way up."

"Wh-wh-wh-wh-wh." I wanted to find out what the business was, but all I could get out was a sound like an engine that wouldn't start.

"You'll be making robes."

I frowned, not understanding.

"At Harcourt's. They are robe makers and tailors. A very well-established business supplying professional garments not only for clergymen, but also for members of the legal and teaching professions. You may not find yourself within the ranks of professional men, son, but you will, at least, have the honor to take their measure, so to speak, and to see them well turned out."

He smiled at me and I ran my hand back through my hair, making it stand on end, as if I'd been hit by lightning, I guess, because he glanced at my hair and his smile turned into a dis-approving scowl.

I wanted to tell him that this line of work was of no inter-est to me, that I loved boats, and the open air, and the locks and charts and maps showing which channels were safe and which ones needed to be marked out. I wanted to explore rivers and lakes, to plot courses and make maps and find my way by myself. But I'd never get it out in a month of Sundays. I made an attempt, but I knew my eyes were bulging and my mouth was skewed every which way. He turned his head away so he wouldn't have to look at me. It was useless.

"Well," he said, standing up, "we don't have to make a decision right now. We have a year to think about it, haven't we? I think, though, that you'll agree that it would be a very fine position. You will learn to measure and cut cloth, and to operate a sewing machine. I can see that you like machinery. You would be out of the way of the general public, which would be easy on your nerves. Quite the ideal position all around! Your life is just beginning, my boy!"

Even though night was falling, I could see satisfaction in his face. He had just solved the big Freddie-problem.

Fireflies appeared, winking at us lazily as if they had other things on their minds than generating light. One came to rest on a tall piece of grass, and I captured it by cupping both hands over it. I held it for a moment watching its pale green glow through my fingers. It flickered more and more slowly, with less and less enthusiasm. I opened my hands to release it, but it sat where it was, not knowing it could make its escape and fly away. I blew at it and off it went.

We sat there for a while longer. Papa said his business would keep him here a few nights. I wondered briefly what that business could be, and then recalled his letter. Maybe he really was going to look for property to buy. I nearly asked him, but didn't. I didn't want to think about any more changes.

It was pretty dark. After wishing me a good night, he headed up in the direction of the cottage and I began to take the short route to our tent, through the trees instead of down along the shore. After a moment I heard him call out, "Frederick? Are you still there?"

I stopped. "Yes," I said.

"I can't seem to find my way in the dark. There's no path."

I went back to him. There is a path of brown pine needles that winds its way between the junipers and the pines and the birch trees right up to the field of daisies, past their prime now, separating the cottage from the shore, but you can't see it at night. You have to let your feet feel it while you get your bearings from the birch trees, which loom out of the darkness like slender ghosts. Hesitantly I took him by the elbow, gently, and guided him through the trees until we could see lamplight from the cottage window. "You must have eyes like a cat," he said. We stood outside in the dark for a moment listening to the others: the boys asking for more hot ginger, Bessie arguing about bedtime, Uncle Will rummaging around looking for mosquito netting so he could sleep out all night in the hammock, and Tom cheering because Grandma said he could sleep on the daybed in the living room to give over his bed to Papa.

"Won't you come in?" Papa said to me, but I shook my head. You can't get your thoughts sorted out if you're constantly listening to other people expressing theirs. I wanted to figure out why I didn't feel as though my life was just beginning. Papa made his way to the veranda, swishing the last of the daisies out of his way, beheading them with his walking stick.

11

Character Building

It started to rain at one o'clock last night and was raining hard when we wakened. We lay in bed and played FLINCH *till ten o'clock. The rain came through the airholes in the top of the tent and, as my boots were underneath them, it formed a little lake in them. A person cannot imagine unless he has been there how chilly and cold it is on the lakeshore, especially on a day like that. We went swimming anyway, in spite of the cold, and got cleaned up. After supper we went to a dance. The dance was exhausting.*

We eventually got tired of playing cards, and Ernie and Harold, wanting a dry breakfast, decided to get dressed and make a buck-dart for the cottage through the rain. I turned on my side and pulled the blankets and quilts up around my ear, and listened to the rain pelting the roof of the tent. I wanted a few more minutes of feeling warm and dry and protected and safe from all entanglements and expectations. I wondered how Papa was faring in this weather. He'd be mighty bored, I guessed. He doesn't play cards and he thinks puzzles are a waste of time. He might read, unless he's already read the books we have here. Auntie Lizzie keeps us supplied with novels, but I don't think he approves of novels unless they're by Mr. Dickens or Mr. Kipling.

Thinking about my father made me think about the future he has planned for me, which caused me to get a pain in my stomach imagining what it would be like to live and work in a large city. I forced my thoughts back to the present time, the present day. It's hard to keep the days straight at the lake because there's no set routine, except for getting up and going to bed and eating three meals somewhere in between. I felt a sudden jolt of excitement. Today was Saturday! The day of the Maberly girls' dance at Rideau Ferry.

Tonight would be the night I would hold Nora in my arms and dance with her with my hand on her waist, her slender waist. And I would press my face close to hers, and breathe in her scent, and perhaps let my lips brush her cheek. And look into her eyes. And she would look lovingly back at me and I would kiss her lips and. . . . I began to shiver and tremble, and rolled myself into a tight ball because I felt like I was dying from the inside out.

"Not sick are you, son?"

Good grief! Papa.

"No," I mumbled into the quilt without looking up. With the rain hammering away at the tent and my brain getting all hot and bothered, and with half my brain fluid ready to disappear, I hadn't even heard his footsteps. If he saw that I was barely awake, he might go away. I opened my eyes a crack and saw him standing all serious and concerned in the tent doorway, with Auntie Lizzie's flowered parasol protecting his brown tweed suit.

"I thought you boys might like to look at some properties with me. Not in the rain, of course, but later if it lets up. I've heard of one or two for sale around here."

"But-but-but. W-w-w-we like it here at Grandpa's." We so seldom argue with him that he's in the habit of not hearing us if we do. He said, "We could borrow one of your grandpa's boats."

"Per-per-per maybe."

"Well, anyway, it's time you were up. A rainy day is no excuse for laziness."

When I looked again, he was gone. He'd never last a weekend at the cottage. He would certainly never last a whole month. He wouldn't be able to leave the town behind him.

In the cottage, I discovered that everybody else seemed to think a rainy day *was* an excuse for laziness. Ettie and Auntie Min were playing cards in the kitchen with the boys; Grandpa was dozing in his rocking chair; Tom was sprawled on the floor building a house with a set of dominoes; Auntie Lizzie was lying on the daybed reading a novel that looked suspiciously unlike anything written by either Mr. Dickens or Mr. Kipling; Bessie was cutting pictures out of the *Family Herald* for her scrapbook; Grandma, with a shawl around her shoulders and another over her knees, was knitting and watching the birds attack a block of suet beaded with seeds outside the window; and Uncle Will was in one of the bedrooms snoring because he'd got rained out of his hammock in the middle of the night.

Papa had been walking back and forth jingling coins in his pocket, but now was standing in the doorway to the veranda looking glumly out at the wall of ivy surrounding it, providing cooling protection from the sun when it shone, but not much of anything when it rained, except the sound of raindrops pit-pattering on the leaves. The only other sounds came from the slapping down of cards in the kitchen, with the occasional groan or cheer, Bessie humming something that didn't seem to have a tune, and from the plink-plink-plink of rain coming in through a leak in the roof and hitting a metal basin placed underneath to catch the drips.

"Well," Papa said when he saw me, "what shall we all do to occupy ourselves today?" Nobody else answered him because they were all pretty well occupied as it was.

I said, "Go swim-swim-swimming."

"It's raining," he said.

"And much too cold," Grandma added.

I said, "I don't mind." And I didn't. Whether anybody else joined me or not, I was going to go for a swim with a hunk of soap to get all shined up for the dance. I even thought about borrowing Uncle Will's razor. I hadn't looked in a mirror for a while, but I could feel a few bristles here and there when I rubbed my jaw and my chin.

"I think all you boys should go for a nice long bathe with some soap," Auntie Lizzie said loudly as if she'd been reading my mind. "If you're going off to a dancing party tonight, you don't want to offend the ladies."

"They won't have the dance if it's raining," Harold called from the kitchen.

We could hear Ettie contradicting him. "They will so. Why do you think umbrellas were invented? Besides, we'll have a roof over our heads and the rain's letting up."

It might have been letting up a little, but it hadn't stopped. It seemed that the moment Grandma said it was too cold for a swim, all the boys decided to go anyway to prove what a tough and hardy lot we were. Although they objected to the piece of soap.

"Come with us, Papa," Ernie said.

"Ho, ho, ho," he laughed, somewhat falsely, I thought. He's not really a ho-ho-ho-ing sort of person. "I didn't come prepared with a bathing costume."

"Borrow mine." Uncle Will had just emerged from the back of the cottage, looking rumpled and sleepy-eyed. He turned his head and I think he winked at me, although he may only have had something in his eye. He was sizing up Papa. "We're about the same build." Papa started to object, but Will said, "Nonsense. Do you the world of good to get out there with your boys. Show 'em how to do the Australian crawl."

"Oh, no, no, no," Papa was saying, with something like joviality. "They don't want me interfering in their high jinks."

"Sure we do," Ernie said. He had got Uncle Will's bather from the nail where it usually hung behind one of the bedroom doors, and handed it to him.

Auntie Lizzie was sitting up now with her book upside down in her lap. She smiled up sweetly at Papa. "What a wonderful opportunity for you to set a good example in character building." Papa looked at her for a long moment, but he didn't actually return her smile. "Anyway," she went on, "you don't want to stay cooped up inside just because of a little rain. We're not very industrious on a rainy day, I'm afraid."

He pulled on his chin looking thoughtful, his expression a little pinched. Grandma said to him, "Now don't you let them talk you into doing something you don't want to do. You look half-frozen to me. You just sit right down beside me." She patted the space on the settee beside her and took the shawl off her knees. "Here, now. Put this around your shoulders and you'll be snug as a bug in no time."

I don't know why Grandma has this effect on people that makes them go right out and do the opposite of what she says. By the time we got outside in the rain in our bathers walking down to the shore, holding our mouths up for drinks of raindrops, Papa had appeared wearing Uncle Will's black wool bathing suit. The vest part was somewhat tight across his stomach, and the attached short trousers came down almost to his knees because he's not quite as tall as Uncle Will, although he's stouter. His arms and legs looked like unscraped parsnips compared to our summer-brown skins, and he was covered with goose pimples. I was beginning to think about plucked chickens instead of parsnips when Tom, looking scared, pulled me off the path and whispered, "He's going to find out I can't swim."

Papa and Ernie and Harold were talking about whether the water would be colder or warmer than the air. Tom and I lagged behind, letting them get ahead of us. I said, "You can swim."

He frowned up at me. "You know I can't."

"You can swim underwater. I saw-saw-saw you do it."

He started to think about this. "That was only because I was drowning," he said.

"But you didn't drown. If-if-if you hadn't been swimming, you'd have sunk like a s-s-s-stone. But you didn't. You were swimming underwater. The only thing you did wrong was-was-was forget to hold your breath."

He was gnawing on both his thumb knuckles, elbows tight to his ribs, looking out from under his rain-soaked hair to watch first Ernie, and then Harold, scoot to the end of the boat dock and, knees tucked up, bombard the lake with a splash. Papa was trying to enclose himself in his own arms to keep from shivering.

I said to Tom, "Wade in up to your neck."

"Yeah," he said, "and then what? Tell him I lied?"

"No. Hold your breath, duck your head under, and start swimming."

"And start drowning, you mean."

"And kee-kee-keep your eyes open." He scowled at me, puzzled. "As long as you keep your eyes open, you wo-wo-wo-won't drown." When Tom grows up he's going to tell people, "My brother used to hand me such a load of bullroar, it's a wonder I'm alive to tell it."

We both got into the water at the shallow end of the dock. Papa stopped hugging himself long enough to wave the other boys back in closer to shore, but they only waved back and kept on horsing around. I stood on the stony bottom about ten feet from Tom and whispered, "Do it." I had my back to Papa so I didn't know whether he was watching or not.

Tom had a look on his face that reminded me of a hooked mudpout: lips turned down, eyes bulging. "Keep your eyes open," I mouthed. "Aim for me. I'll grab you." He put his hands together in front of his nose, which I have an idea meant he was saying a quick prayer, ducked his head, kicked up his heels, and, before I knew it, he was grabbing my swimming pants. I pulled him up.

"I did it!" he screamed. "I was swimming! Did you see me swimming?" he yelled at Papa. Harold and Ernie plowed through the water toward us to see what all the fuss was about. "I was swimming!" he screeched in their direction.

"Very nice," Papa said. "Now let's see you do a dive."

Tom had his mudpout look again, but the other boys punched his shoulder and messed up his hair and said, "Pip-pip" and "Good going," and pretty soon he was saying, "I coulda swam about a mile only Freddie got in my way."

Ernie and Harold climbed out and started coaxing Papa in. "It's warmer in than out," Ernie said.

"I have no doubt, but it's still too cold for me."

"Come on," they begged. They each had him by an arm at the deep end of the dock, pulling him toward the edge; and he was laughing in that un-Papa-like ho-ho way he'd taken up, struggling against them, pulling back, trying to swing his arms free. Tom climbed out and started pushing from behind. "Now, now, boys," Papa said. "I'll go in at the shallow end in my own time. Whoa there! Whoa!" he yelled.

When I thought about it, that's my only memory of his swimming in the past – wading in the shallow water up to his waist and getting out again because he was cold.

Harold and Ernie were pulling at only about half-strength, I could tell. My father isn't a very big man. If they'd wanted, they could have tossed him ten feet out, although I don't think they ever would have. But with Tom pushing from behind, things got a little out of hand. I had swum out a piece, watching. The expression on Papa's face stopped being mock-jovial and started being terrified as he got closer and closer to the edge of the dock. "Stop! Let me go!" he screamed. At that same instant Tom gave a last boisterous shove, and Ernie and

Harold, taking pity on Papa, stopped pulling and let him go. From where I was, ten feet out, it looked like he was flapping his arms like wings trying to fly. He couldn't stop himself. Just before he broke the surface, his face looked like Tom's had when he fell out of the boat: his mouth a shocked O and his eyes staring up, nearly all white, getting a glimpse of death. That's how I knew he couldn't swim.

I churned through the water toward him, hand over hand. His head came up to the surface, and he spluttered and coughed and flailed his arms. Just as he was going down again, I grabbed him, keeping his head up, and dragged him into shallower water, and I thought, he doesn't seem to weigh any more than Tom.

He stood in the shallow water coughing, trying to get his breath, not looking at anyone, so I said, "You must have tak-tak-taken a cramp."

Ernie, looking scared out of his wits, gave him a hand up as he tried, weakly, to climb out of the water onto the dock.

"Sorry, Papa," he said.

Tom was shivering, with his knuckles up to his mouth again, waiting as we all were, for a stern lecture. But Papa didn't say a word. He rubbed water from his eyes with the heels of his hands, ran his fingers back through his hair to tidy it, and said only, "Too cold to suit me." We watched him pick his way on tender feet along the path up toward the cottage.

"I didn't know your father couldn't swim," Harold said.

"He took a cramp," Ernie said, looking at me. I didn't say

anything. I looked down at my legs and feet in the water, all stubby and wavery, looking too short to support me. The lake can be deceiving.

Harold said, "I always used to think he could do everything, probably better than everybody else." He started along the rocky shore to the tent. Ernie followed and I heard him say, "It was just a cramp. Anybody can take a cramp."

I climbed out of the water onto the dock where Tom stood all shivering and blotchy, with raindrops splashing off his shoulders. "I never knew he couldn't swim," he said.

"Not a crime," I said.

Auntie Lizzie was coming down the path with her flowery umbrella. "Everything all right?" she called.

"Yes, ma'am."

"I thought your father looked a little pale."

"May-may-maybe it was the shock of the cold water."

"Quite likely." She turned back to get in out of the rain.

12

If Wishes Were Horses

Yesterday was Sunday and we all slept in until after nine. We spent a lazy morning reading in the grove. Grandma, Auntie Lizzie, and Auntie Min read their Bibles for half an hour and then Auntie Min started asking about the dance we attended the night before. Ettie and Bessie talked themselves hoarse about it. Tom said it was stupid, and Ernie and Harold said it was swell if you like that sort of thing.

Before noon, Uncle Will offered to take everyone for a ride in the *Bessie*. I said I wanted to stay in the grove and read, and then Papa declined in favor of helping Grandma shell peas for dinner. Everyone else went in the boat. I put up the hammock and read an interesting book recommended by Grandpa until dinnertime. Papa kept walking past me, but I was reading so much I didn't notice him until he was well past.

Sometimes you think you're reading along, getting down toward the bottom of the page, and then you realize you haven't taken in any of it, that you've been thinking thoughts of your own. The more I read, the more this kept happening to me. I was thinking about the day before yesterday and how after our chilly swim, Auntie Lizzie told us boys to take a brush to our good clothes and lay them out for the dance.

The rain had let up, and pretty soon the sun came out and we were able to hang our clothes out on the chokecherry bushes behind the tent for a good airing. By supper time everyone was talking about the dance as if it were the biggest event of our lives. We were so used to leading our free and easy cottage lives, I guess, that something as civilized as a dance threw us all into a tizzy.

Ettie said, how could she go dancing when she didn't have one decent thing to wear, and she might as well stay home because who wants to go out where people can see you looking like a frump. Auntie Lizzie said she had three little bows she could sew onto her white shirtwaist that would look just darling, and who would know that it wasn't brand-new, and with a nice bright smile on her face, she'd be the belle of the ball.

Ettie said, "Oh, Mother!"

Auntie Min said she'd stay home and write letters because she was too old to attend these juvenile revelries. Ettie said,

"Don't be such a chump, Min." And Min said, "I have to catch up on my correspondence." And Ettie wanted to know who she was writing to, and Min said, "Why, our friend Mr. McAlpine. Has he not written to you?" Ettie's eyes flashed and she said, "That cad! I hope he never does, for I'll tear it up." And Min said, "Temper, temper!" And Auntie Lizzie muttered, "My daughter and my sister will undoubtedly be the death of me," and went out to the outhouse and slammed the door and didn't come back in for half an hour.

We boys cooked ourselves an elephant supper, bananas and pork and beans being on the list, and Auntie Lizzie said we shouldn't have had pork and beans when we're going out to a party, and Tom asked why not, but nobody felt like telling him in front of Papa.

Uncle Will said, "I think Fred could be in charge of taking all the young people in the *Bessie*." I felt myself grow about ten inches, right on the spot. Uncle Will looked over at Papa, who was reading a two-day-old paper and turning the pages fast, rustling them loudly, so that we were all aware that he was put out with the lack of fresh news. "Unless you have any objections," he said to Papa. Papa looked up to see about eight pairs of eyes staring at him and one pair of lips, Bessie's, murmuring, "Please-please-please-please."

"I have no objections," he said, "provided he's aware of the enormous responsibility." He was looking hard at me now, peering closely to see if I showed even a glimmer of awareness. I felt my eyes growing rounder and stupider-looking, and my neck getting red and itchy. And at the same time I had the feeling that he was pleased to see me doing this. He seemed satisfied that nothing had changed.

I said, "Y-y-y-yes, sir." I tried to get rid of the idea of his being satisfied because he's my father after all. He likes us to respect him. But it stuck like a gramophone needle in a cracked record. I looked down so that I wouldn't have to see that familiar look on his face, and he said, "Son, you're going to have to learn to look other men in the eye if you're ever going to make your way in this world."

I got us up to Rideau Ferry without a hitch. Harold's nose was out of joint because I was asked to be the captain, not him, even though he's six months older, and he kept making disparaging remarks about my ability to operate the boat. When he saw the slick landing I made at the Rideau Ferry wharf, slipping neatly in between a rowboat and another launch already tied up, he had to let out a whistle. We tied up, bow and stern, and made our way up to the hotel, where the dance was being held. There were quite a few buggies out front, backed tight to the fence that ran between the hotel lawn and the road. The horses all faced the road so they wouldn't be tempted to bite people strolling beside the hotel.

From inside, we could hear the band playing something that sounded like an Irish jig, and I began to feel all jumpy on the inside and sweaty on the outside because, how the heck are you supposed to dance to an Irish jig? I turned and loped back down to the lake to make sure we really had tied up the boat and that I hadn't just imagined it. The boat was tied.

There was a veranda around the hotel lighted by colored lanterns and, inside the ballroom, electric lamps here and there along the walls gave enough light to make the girls look glamorous and the young men look like titled gentlemen.

As soon as we walked in, we were greeted by Nora and her sister, Edna. Nora shone in a dress the color of a summer sky in the early evening. She had swept her hair up and piled it on top of her head, and looked as regal as a queen. We all shook hands with Nora and with Edna, who seemed jolly enough, but who couldn't hold a candle to Nora. Then we were introduced to a lot of ladies, who were there as chaperones, and to one or two gentlemen, including their elderly friend.

"This is Mr. Adams," Edna said. He looked happier now than he had when last we saw him in the village of Newboro. We shook hands with him.

People were walking about, talking to each other and lining up at the refreshment table for little cups of something pink. Bessie clung to Ettie, and the two of them started chatting to other girls Ettie knew, who bent over and made a big fuss over Bessie. She was in her element.

Tom said he would stay for exactly ten minutes, and then he was going to go back and sit in the boat and wait there until it was time to go home. I took out my watch and saw that it was going to be a long evening.

The band struck up a waltz then, and pretty soon lots of

fellows were asking girls to dance. The dance floor filled up
with swirling couples: some bumping into others, some stumbling awkwardly as if they weren't exactly experts. Ernie and
Harold and I leaned against the wall and made hilarious
remarks behind our hands about some of the stumblebums.
We laughed a lot, even at remarks that weren't particularly
funny. The whole time, though, I knew exactly where Nora
was. I saw Wilf go up to her and bow like a royal swell and
take her by the hand, and out they went to the middle of the
dance floor where he could be the center of attention.
Everyone, however, was looking at Nora.

Tom said, "See you later. I'm going to sit in the boat." But
he only got as far as the refreshment table and came back to
tell us he'd heard there were to be eats later on. "I might as
well wait till they bring them out. No sense having them go
to waste."

Nora was dancing with someone else now: a tall fellow,
who held her a bit too close, I thought. She can't like that very
well in a warm room like this. What a numbskull!

Maybe I should ask her to dance. I definitely would as soon
as the band started up again after this set. She seemed to be
looking around as if she was searching for someone, and
glancing at the door to see who was coming in or going out.
Maybe she was looking for me to see if I was dancing with
anyone. It was entirely possible.

Edna and two other girls swooped down on us out of
nowhere. Edna said, "We have orders from the chaperones to

ask all the wallflowers to dance." Edna pulled me by the coat sleeve out toward the dance floor, and the other girls similarly attacked Ernie and Harold. As soon as Tom saw what was up, he darted for the opposite end of the room.

I shuffled across the floor pushing Edna in front of me like a broom, more or less in time with the music. "Are you having a nice time?" she asked. I said, "Swell," and made an about-turn to sweep her back again to the starting line. "There's Nora," she said. "What say we bump into them?"

"B-b-bump into them?"

"Yes. She hates when people don't watch where they're going. She needs livening up. She's starting to mope."

"L-l-let's not."

Before I could do anything, Edna had taken the lead, forcing me to turn into the thick of the dancers, and was trundling me along toward Nora, who had her head turned away from her partner, stretching her neck, peering around. Edna took aim and, with an almighty swing, heaved her rear end into Nora's hip, practically knocking her off her pins.

"Awfully sorry," Edna said. Nora's partner helped her recover her balance. Nora wrinkled her nose at her sister and called her a hussy. Edna laughed and said, "Better that than a dead fish. Cheer up. You're spoiling the party." Nora ignored the remark and introduced her partner, Rowland something.

I was barely listening to their chitchat because I was thinking about some book I'd read where a person cut right in on someone dancing and danced away with the girl, and that's exactly what I would do, right this minute. Couples spun past, sidestepping us as I started to say, "M-m-m-may," but realized Edna hadn't stopped talking to Nora. She said, "I've asked the band to play a couple of reels and maybe a square dance if we can get someone to call off."

"Square dancing will be too rough."

"But this is too tiresome."

"May I-I-I-I," I tried again.

"Don't be ridiculous. Everyone's having fun, I believe."

Nora's partner looked glazed with boredom; Nora herself looked distraught with two red spots high on her cheeks; and Edna looked bursting with energy as if the only fun to be had would be in kicking up her heels.

"C-c-c-c-cut. . . ." They all stared at me as if I had swallowed a fish bone and was trying to cough it up.

"Pardon?" Rowland said.

I reached out for Nora with both hands as if I would grab her and sling her over my shoulder like a sack of potatoes. Fortunately, just at that moment, she caught on. "Are you cutting in?" she asked. I nodded and she grinned impishly. "That's the first time I've ever had anyone cut in. Gosh, he's brave, isn't he?" she said to old Rowland. "You don't mind, do you?"

He shrugged and reached out to take Edna's hand at the exact moment I started to take Nora's, and old Rowly and I nearly ended up in each other's arms. The band was still playing something romantic and kind of slow, and I put my hand on Nora's waist exactly the way Ettie had shown me. My other hand shot up like a train signal and Nora reached out and took it and, before we knew it, we were swaying rapturously, moving our feet here and there and dancing more or less like everyone else. Little by little I inched my hand around to her back and squeezed her closer because there were so many people around us you could hardly dance together and keep a respectable distance, I told myself.

I wanted to dance with my cheek against hers, but this was impossible as she was about half a head taller. I wanted to look into her eyes. I read somewhere about people speaking volumes with their eyes and I had thought, at the time, that that was something I should take up as I have so much trouble even speaking sentences with my mouth. But her gaze had drifted to the door again.

I gave her hand a quick squeeze, and she looked at me. "Sorry," she said, "did you say something?" I tried to make my eyes go all soft and loving to show her my true feelings, but she looked alarmed and said, "Are you all right?" I nodded. By now I probably looked a little sad because things weren't working out the way I had hoped they would. She said, "Have you ever been in love, Fred?"

My eyes opened wide. I nodded vigorously.

"Isn't it awful?"

I nodded again. I wished I could say something easily about being in love and how I had this raging passion going on inside me, boiling up, just barely locked in.

"You feel so incomplete," she said, "don't you think?" (I must have nodded.) "Like something's missing." She was looking dreamily into the air above my head and seemed to be talking to herself. "Like some poor boat dragged into the middle of a grassy field, no water within a mile. Do you know what I mean?"

"I know," I said. I was starting to notice how girls spend a lot of time talking about how they feel instead of showing it. It was all I could do to keep from pulling her face down close to mine and squashing my lips onto hers to show her all about love. I wanted to pull her in closer because I wanted to see how her curves felt right up against me, but the music stopped and she let go of me to clap for the band along with everyone else. "That was lovely, Fred," she said. "Thank you for cutting in. It perked me right up." She wiggled her fingers in a good-bye and started walking outside to the veranda. I felt as if my breathing apparatus had quit on me. After a moment I followed her out. From inside I could hear one of the chaperones announcing a square dance after the break.

I saw her at the end of the veranda, half sitting on the railing, leaning her head against a post, looking out over the expanse of lawn and the water beyond it. Above, the sky had reached that in-between stage: not quite light, but not yet dark, clinging to the gloaming until the last possible moment. Far across the lake, above the tree line, the first star glimmered shyly and I felt like making a wish on it, but didn't.

All right, I did. Sometimes things come into your head,

even when you tell yourself over and over, I'm not going to think about that. *Star light, star bright, first star I see tonight* came into my head and wouldn't leave. *Wish I may, wish I might, have this wish I wish tonight.* It was something my mother and I used to say, about a hundred years ago.

I wished I had the nerve to tell Nora I loved her. That's all. If I told her, I'm pretty sure she would be obliged to say it back. That's how it works in some of Auntie Lizzie's novels, at any rate. The girls are just waiting for it, pining for the fellow to say, "I love you."

A breeze was rising, rustling through the leaves above the hotel. She didn't hear me making my way toward her, passing a couple with their arms around each other's waists and their heads close together; and another couple further along the railing standing apart from each other, their heads pointing in opposite directions – a lover's quarrel, I imagined. Nora stood up suddenly and I stopped where I was. I looked out over the lawn. Nothing much to see. Three young men smoking; old Mr. Adams putting his pipe away, bending over his cane, trudging up the lawn toward the veranda steps; a girl tying another girl's hair ribbon. Out on the lake I could see a rowboat with a lot of people in it and, closer to shore, someone paddling a canoe toward the Rideau Ferry wharf.

The old man, cane on one side, leaned heavily on the stair rail, pulling himself one step at a time up the veranda steps just as Nora skimmed down them, barely noticing him. She turned her head at the bottom and said something to him, and then stood with her back to the hotel on a rise of lawn, her skirt billowing in the breeze, her hair where it had come undone a little, feathering her neck and cheek. I stood near the top step, waiting, watching her waiting. Mr. Adams rumbled "Good evening" to me and sank with a thud into one of the wicker chairs lining the wall behind me.

I was making up my mind whether to go down to where she stood, deserted, isolated in the middle of the lawn. I could almost feel the old man's eyes watching me watching her, but I didn't care. I went down a step and down again as a young man in shirtsleeves carrying his jacket came up from the wharf. Nora's back straightened and her chin rose as he approached. He stood in front of her, taking both her hands in his, holding them. I could hear his voice, but couldn't make out what he said. I felt something inside me collapse and drop dead.

They strolled, their arms entwined, hands clasped. She kept looking up at him and he looked down at her every so often, smiling. There was something sneaky about his lips, I thought, half-hidden as they were by his mustache. As they moved up the lawn, he cocked a salute to the fellows smoking and, after they'd passed the two girls fixing each other's hair bows, he turned to stare at them.

They were heading right for me where I stood halfway down the steps. I turned to scramble up them, out of sight, stumbling as I did, tripping over my own big feet. I smashed my knee against the edge of the top step and felt like yelling, but I groaned instead and darted behind the wide corner post where I was more or less out of sight.

I heard the fellow reply to something Nora said, "Now I really am jealous."

"And that's not all," she said. "Someone cut in while I was dancing with him."

"Where is he? I'll turn him into mincemeat."

"Silly! He's only a sweet boy. Wilf and I surprised him skinny-dipping early one morning."

Pins and needles pierced my entire body.

"He was swimming naked in front of you?"

"Diving, in fact. It was very educational."

"Nora, you're a holy terror!"

Every square inch of my body went numb.

They were nearing the steps. I watched the fellow pull her into the shadows below me, away from the colored lanterns, and bend over her, drawing her close, kissing her – gently at first, and then with so much feeling that I knew my insides weren't completely dead after all. For one quivering moment I thought it was me kissing her, and then my heart did a swan dive that ended in a splat on something hard, maybe my ribs, or maybe the rock that I seemed to have developed inside me, weighing me down.

They drifted past me, barely seeing me, eyes only for each other. My knee hurt so much I felt like crying. When they had gone in, I limped over to one of the wicker chairs and sat down, two over from the old man. So, all along, she'd known it was me. I slouched, resting my head against the chair back, hands in my pockets, legs straight out in front. I was exhausted, supremely tired of my life, which was just as well, because I figured it was over. Lord! Stitch stark naked!

Inside my pocket I closed my hand over my watch and pulled it out attached to its chain. I popped the lid open. It wasn't very late. Not quite nine. I thought I should take it and smash it against something to make time stop right here. Summer 1904. The end.

13

After the Ball Is Over

Yesterday, Auntie Min also asked me if I'd had a good time at the dance, but I just flicked my hand in a so-so kind of answer because I was absorbed in the book I was reading. It is hard to describe just how numbing a dance can be.

Sunday was an abnormally long day, as I recall. In the afternoon Ernie said, "You shouldn't read all day, you know. You'll ruin your eyes." I was sitting in the *Jumbo* inside the boathouse with an open book in my lap, the one I had been reading in the grove that morning. "Come on, we're going to give Mr. Buchanan a hand at the locks." But I shook my head and stayed where I was, turning pages, until I saw Papa coming down the path toward me. At that exact moment I decided to take the *Jumbo* out and row across the lake to explore the opposite shore. I untied it, rowing hard, looking over my shoulder to correct my direction. By the time Papa made his way into the boathouse, I was well out from shore. If he called me, I didn't hear him.

Rowing a boat is good for the muscles. It took me thirty-three minutes to get across the lake, and then I spent an hour and twenty-five minutes rowing along the south shore. There aren't many cottages over there, mostly farmers' fields where cows come down to the lake to drink, and groves of trees, and shoreline rocks layered and stacked like platters. I fished for a while, but didn't catch anything, probably because my heart wasn't in it. I think you really have to want to catch fish before they'll bite.

I got thinking about how you reach a point near the end of the summer where you feel you've had enough, and you wouldn't mind sitting in front of a roaring good fire, listening to the wind howl outside, watching the snow swirl madly around the window, and you know nothing is expected of you except to sit tight and wait out the storm. This is what I was thinking as I squinted into the dazzling sun, sweat rolling down my face like tears.

I was willing to think about almost anything except what was most on my mind. I felt flattened, as if all the events of the summer were layered and stacked on top of me, crushing me, splitting me open, with part of me here pulling hard on the oars, part of me still back in Saturday night, and part of me heading out of sight into the dim future.

Sitting on the hotel veranda while time hung in the air refusing to move forward, I thought, I can't get much lower than this. The old man had noticed me pull my watch out of my pocket and kept staring at me.

"Fine-lookin' watch you have there, son."

Hunched like a gnome, he was waiting for me to say something. With an effort I began, "It-it-it was a . . ."

"Speak up, lad."

"Pr-pr-pr gift from my father," I said as loudly as I could. I wished he would go away or take a weak turn or something, and leave me to my wretchedness. I was thinking I should join a monastery where they have these vows of silence and I could live there for the rest of my miserable life. I'm not a Catholic, though. Another door banged shut in my face.

"May I see it?" He set glasses on the end of his nose.

I undid the clasp and handed it over. He held it up to the light coming through the window behind him, squinting at the inscription around the edge. TIME DISCOVERS TRUTH, he read. "Do you believe that?" His voice rasped.

I hadn't thought much about it, but I nodded.

"Of course you do." He took off the pince-nez. "Every passing minute reveals some new truth about ourselves or about those around us. Trouble is, it's hard on us. We can only take so much truth." He choked, coughing, unable to get his breath. He put a handkerchief over his mouth and spat. I wished Wilf would come along and take him home. From inside I could hear a violin tuning up as a fiddle for the square dance.

"You must be very fond of him."

"Wh-wh-who?"

He handed back the watch. "Your father."

I sat bent over my knees, my chin in my hand. I tried hard to think about the honest truth and muttered, "N-n-n-not al-al-al-ways."

"What's that, son? Speak up."

"I-I-I-I." It's hard to shout and stutter at the same time, and I was still thinking about what was true and what wasn't. I found myself saying, "I guess I am."

I'm not even sure he heard me. He nodded his head vigorously and stared at the floor as if he saw something horrible there. "I, too, was given a watch when I was about your age."

I said something like, "Oh."

"Stolen!" He spit the word. I could see the muscles of his face clenching and unclenching.

"P-p-pardon?"

"And so I gave it back. Oh, indeed I did. I gave him back what he deserved." He turned in my direction, staring, eyes like live coals. I wondered if I should go looking for Wilf.

In the next moment his voice became calm. "Never had what you'd call a real father."

I didn't want to encourage this. "Mm," I said.

"What's that?"

"MM."

The wicker seat of his chair creaked as he settled himself more comfortably. "Yes, sir, that's a very nice watch you have. Time passing is what keeps life bearable," he said. "It doesn't always help you forget, but it makes remembering less painful. I wonder why that is?"

"DUNNO."

I could hear him pull in each breath and blow it out noisily. "Oh, I had a father, of course. Everybody has a father. But not everybody knows his father was the devil incarnate. I do."

I turned to look at him, making my own chair crunch. His chin was nearly on his chest, but his eyes blazed up from under a snowy hedge of eyebrow. "May he roast in hell!" he growled. A vein at his temple bulged and throbbed. "And do you know what I did?" he shouted, his voice vibrating. "I ran away to forget the wickedness. And now, in my old age, it creeps back to haunt me. I had hoped to die in peace, had hoped for the blessing of total forgetfulness. But, there you are," he muttered, "time discovers truth. And I am no better than he was."

"It's chilly out here, Grandfather. Best come inside." Wilf had appeared out of the shadows. He helped old Mr. Adams to his feet. To me he said, "Grandfather has violent nightmares and sometimes he thinks they really happened." He tried to take the old man's arm, but his grandfather turned to me. "My cane," he said. It was leaning against the chair beside me. I handed it to him. "What time is it now, lad?" he asked.

I opened my watch again. "Ten after nine," I told him. Quietly he said, "You're beginning to forget her already, I'll wager."

The old man left, leaning on Wilf's arm, and I stayed out on the veranda for a while, wishing I were a hundred miles away instead of sprawled in a wicker chair, listening to someone call off the square dance moves, his voice as twangy as catgut pulled to breaking point. "Swing yer pairtners ra-ound and ra-ound, ella-min layft in yer carners all." At one point I stood up to stretch and looked through the window in time to see Nora take Tom by the arm and swing him almost off his feet. Her beau stood on the sidelines watching, grinning, stroking his silly mustache. They did a do-si-do as smart as anything, backing into their places in the square to clap in time to the music while Ernie and Edna went into the center.

And a rare old time was had by all, I said to myself.

I watched through the window for a moment longer, feeling foreign, like an explorer visiting a strange land, observing the natives, understanding their language, but unable to speak it. If I were Stanley, I would write in my journal: "The natives of this land don't have a care in the world. They know they belong with one another like one huge family and are as happy as the day is long. I am the only outcast."

The square dance ended and soon Ettie came out. She walked along the veranda and sat down beside me on the edge of a chair. "It's hot in there," she said.

I said, "Mm."

We could hear the frogs singing from somewhere behind the hotel. After a little while Ettie reached out and put her hand lightly on my shoulder. She pulled it back when I looked at her, but I noticed a sort of softness around her eyes. After a moment she said, "She was too old for you anyway, Freddie. Didn't you know how old she was?" She put her hand on my sleeve.

"Who?"

"Don't play the innocent. I know you were in love with Nora." I jerked out from under her hand and bent forward, elbows on my knees. Still am, I thought, ridiculous as that may seem.

"She's practically engaged." I turned to stare at her. "At least, so she told me in the strictest confidence. She took me aside and said that next time I saw her, she would most likely be engaged."

"Who to?"

"That chap she's with, of course."

Maybe Ettie doesn't know what "strictest confidence" means. I certainly could have lived without that piece of information.

"She's twenty, you know."

I said, "She does-does-doesn't act twenty."

Ettie encouraged me to go back inside and after a while, I did. The band was playing slow, romantic music again and nearly everyone was dancing. I could see Bessie having a whale of a time dancing with Nora's beau. She was standing on his toes while he wove his way among the dancers, smooth as a snake through grass, his mustache hiding his mean, pink lips. Soon he dumped Bessie for Nora, and Bessie's lower lip fell almost to her boots. Nora was too busy smiling up at her beau to notice.

Maybe I should cut in again, I thought. Maybe I should waltz her right out the door and whisk her down into the *Bessie* boat and turn it straight into the silvery path of the moon, and she'd be so taken with boating in the moonlight that she'd say, *Let's not ever go back*. And we wouldn't.

Then I thought, we'll run out of gasoline eventually, and then what?

Ernie was dancing with Edna, stumbling quite a bit, but she didn't seem to mind. She had her head back laughing, and Ernie was looking pleased with himself. I hoped that Ernie wasn't falling for her. She was pretty old. She wasn't as old as Nora, but gee, Ernie was just a kid. Harold was dancing, too, with his rear end stuck way out and his arm pumping up and down. I thought, I'll imitate him someday when he's trying to get my goat.

I glanced around the room and noticed the refreshment table, now covered with trays of tiny little sandwiches for people with tiny little mouths to nibble on – Nora's gent, for instance. There was Tom, though, who has a good-sized mouth on him for his age, doing his best to see that nothing went to waste. When the music stopped, I got Ernie's eye and Harold's, and they signaled yes when I pointed my thumb toward the door. Well, Harold did. I think Ernie would have stayed talking and laughing with Edna for the rest of the evening, but he tore himself away. I asked Ettie if she wanted to go, but she was with some chap who begged her not to leave. She said she'd find a ride home so I rounded up Bessie and Tom and took one last look around the room.

Nora, alone for the moment, was standing not far from me, near a window, swishing a fan back and forth. Tom and Bessie ran ahead of me out the door and, for a moment, I stood in the doorway looking at Nora. The dancers, most of them, were swarming around the sandwiches, taking a break, so that it almost seemed that we were alone. No one came between us to block my view of her. She turned from the window and saw me standing there, staring sadly at her. She smiled at me, but I didn't have the heart to smile back.

They talk about a person's heart breaking, but mine didn't. It kept on working. I could feel it thumping away inside my chest as strong as ever as I looked at her. It was something else that was broken. I kept thinking about fragile things like the wings of mayflies flitting over the water. She'd taken my dream and pulled it apart, separating me from it. I stood there like a stone and felt myself sinking.

She raised her hand a little to wave at me, but when she

noticed that I wasn't waving back, her eyes got round and serious and she stopped smiling. Her hand came slowly to her mouth as if something had just dawned on her. It was the look of a person who's been careless and only just noticed the damage.

I felt crumpled standing there, knowing I should leave, but not quite able to get my feet to cooperate. Our eyes held for an instant longer. I didn't want her to see tears coming into mine so I turned and made myself walk away.

I walked across the hotel lawn awash in moonlight and ran a sleeve quickly across my eyes. I could hear Ernie and Harold catching up to me. Bessie and Tom were ahead of us, already down on the wharf. "Well, that's that," Ernie said, waving a dismissal in the general direction of the hotel. "Now we can get back to the way we were."

"Wha-wha-what do you mean by that?"

"No more women," he said.

Bessie stood on the wharf, arms folded across her chest. She called out, "This is just ridiclious! You're such a spoil-sport, Freddie!"

I got into the boat and lifted her down in. Tom, half-asleep, staggered in and nabbed the front seat beside the steering wheel, and Harold and Ernie untied the ropes. "The dance isn't even over yet," Bessie yawned. "I'm not even tired." The seat cushions were damp with dew, but we sat on them anyway. "I don't see why Ettie gets to stay," Bessie said. "I hate sitting on wet seats."

"It won't kill you."

"How will Ettie get home?"

"Swim," Harold said.

"She's got a r-r-ride with some friends."

Ernie lit the lantern and held it for me while I primed the engine and got it running smoothly. He said, "Tomorrow we'll go for a rattling good sail, if the wind comes up – you and me and Harold. And Tom, if he wants to."

"And me," Bessie said, but he ignored her.

"Just like we always do," Ernie said. "No more dancing for us. No more romances. We'll build our raft one of these days and load it up with a ton of food and put up our tent on it, and just go wherever the wind takes us and never come back."

"Till winter," Bessie contributed.

"It will never *be* winter and we'll always be this age," Ernie said firmly.

"We'll want an outhouse," Bessie said.

"You'll have one," Harold said, "because you'll be at home with the women."

She stuck out her tongue.

We were chugging through the water now under the almost-full moon, which threw a path across the lake at right angles to us. Tom was beside me in the bow, leaning on his arm on the gunwale, almost asleep. The lantern was fixed to the bow deck. Behind us, sitting between Ernie and Harold, Bessie was trying to make them understand how impossible their dream was. "And who will wash your clothes and mend them for you?"

"We won't wear any."

"And Nora will see you and tell."

I felt a familiar flush of embarrassment. My swan dive must now have reached news bulletin status. How could she do it, tell everyone? How could I still love someone who would do that?

14

Animal Fear

Today we had a game of football. Tom and I stood Ernie and Harold and after a very fast game, Tom and I beat the other fellows 5 goals to 3. It was ripping. When Uncle Will went back to town in the buggy with Grandma, he left me in charge of the Bessie *boat. Harold is none too pleased about that, but he'll get over it. Grandpa says we should make the most of what's left of the summer.*

Sometimes I think Ernie would like to communicate by osmosis because he finds it hard to talk about personal things. Ever since my solitary row across the lake the day after the dance, he's been trying to read my mind. In fact he was down at the boathouse that day waiting for me when I got back. "What took you so long?" he asked.

"Nothing."

He was studying me as if I had some secret map leading to the inside of my mind printed on my forehead. If I told him I'd gone all the way across the lake for the sole purpose of thinking about how heartless women can be, and how treacherous, he'd figure I was barmy. He'd probably say, *You can get that thought over with before you even get out of the boathouse.*

"Papa's been quizzing me," he said.

"What about?"

"He was wondering why you went off in the *Jumbo* by yourself?"

"What did you tell-tell-tell him?" I could see him out of the corner of my eye trying to look into my face, but I turned to tie the boat and then got back in it to get my fishing rod out.

"I told him you wanted to strengthen your arm muscles by rowing. Then he said he thought you seemed different, not yourself."

"I wonder what he meant by that?"

"You seem older."

"Bound to happen." With or without his say-so, I was thinking, but didn't say it to Ernie. I believe Ernie thinks Papa is like a king. You accept everything he does or says with a bow or a salute. I do, too, I guess, because right then I felt like I was committing treason.

Old Mr. Adams was right about time passing making remembering less painful. After a day or two, my vision of Nora waiting for someone disappeared, and my memory of her kissing her beau became as indistinct as if I had seen it through a rain-streaked window fogged by my breath.

After supper Auntie Lizzie reminded us that we hadn't had a bonfire for a while. "Your Papa might enjoy a fine concert," she said. The thought of singing in front of Papa made my throat sore. I told her I couldn't on account of yelling too much playing football.

She leveled her eyes at me, studying me, not believing, but I managed to duck away down to the boathouse before she could press the issue. There were some snarls in my fishing line that needed my attention. I hadn't been there very long before I heard footsteps on the catwalk surrounding it and Papa, bending his neck in the doorway, peered into the gloom. "Isn't it pretty mosquitoey down here?"

"N-n-not too bad."

"I wonder if you'd do me a favor, son?"

I said I would, and he asked me to take him across the lake in the boat to look at a piece of property he'd heard was for sale. "A customer of mine, a Mr. James, told me about it. It's up near Rideau Ferry. There's even a house or cabin on it, of sorts. I wouldn't mind having a look at it while I'm in the neighborhood."

I wasn't exactly in the mood for this, but I agreed. "Shouldn't we-we-we invite the others?" I asked.

"Yes, I guess we should," he said. He went back up to call them while I got the boat in running order.

Sitting up front with my hands on the steering wheel, playing idly with its spokes, I could feel my father's eyes boring into my back, noting my posture, checking the back of my neck for a gray ring. I turned quickly to see what his expression was, but he was looking at the shoreline. He was in the seat behind me with Ernie; Harold and Tom sat behind them. Bessie was up front with me. When we got close to the old Oliver place he leaned forward and said, "I think that's it, there."

I said over my shoulder, "Couldn't be. Tha-tha-that place already has a buyer."

"How do you know?"

"Heard some-some-somebody say so."

"No, I think you must be wrong. Mr. James said it was for sale and was across from Rideau Ferry where the lake narrows, not far from the bridge, and there's apparently an old cabin on it. He said it might be worth fixing up. This looks like the place he described."

Ernie cleared his throat and said loudly over the sound of the engine, "Fred's right. Somebody was looking to buy it, but they may have backed out."

Harold had his ears open and added his two cents' worth. "If you buy it, you'll have to tear the cabin down. It's too run-down and too small to live in."

"I don't suppose you know where the owner lives," Papa said.

I said, "No"; Ernie said, "Yes"; and Harold for once held his tongue. "He's staying at the hotel at Rideau Ferry," Ernie said.

I turned to face Papa. "It-it-it's been sold, prob-prob-prob. Most likely."

"Well, it wouldn't hurt to inquire, anyway, in the event that you might have made a mistake."

I shrugged and steered the boat on past the place. I thought if we rode a little way up the lake, some other property might take his fancy. I slowed down to go under the bridge. "Little Sir Echo, how do you do?" Bessie sang as she always does when we go under the bridge. There isn't really an echo, but the engine always sounds tinny and our voices hollow, for that brief second or two. "HELLO, hello, HELLO, hello," she continued to sing. "Little Sir Echo, how do you do? HELLO . . ."

"Thank you, Bessie," Papa said. "That will do for now. I'd like to be able to hear myself think."

I saw her chin go down and her lower lip go out so I nudged her and mouthed the word "HELLO," and she mouthed, "hello," and I whispered, "HELLO" and we kept this going the correct number of times until we got to the part where she sang in a whisper: "Won't you come over and play? You're a nice little fellow I know by your voice, but you're always so far away. AWAY . . ." She nudged me to be the echo now, and I obliged until Papa poked me in the back to turn around and go back to Rideau Ferry. Slowly I made a sweeping turn and headed back in the direction we'd come. I was planning out my course of action. If I saw any sign of Nora when we got close to the Rideau Ferry dock, I would go right on by and let Papa rant and rave till he turned purple. Almost immediately, I changed my mind because whether I liked it or not, Nora was a fact of life. Like bad-tasting medicine. I thought, if I meet her, I'll close my eyes and swallow fast. We saw no one we knew, however, and I slowed down and made one of the world's greatest landings.

We sat for a moment waiting for a directive from Papa. "Wait here," he said. Ernie and Harold sat on the dock with their legs in the boat to hold it. Papa went up to inquire at the hotel for Mr. Adams. In a few minutes we saw him come back across the lawn. "He wants to talk business down here where it's more private, apparently," Papa said, looking doubtfully at the assortment of fishermen unloading their gear from a boat, young women strolling arm in arm, and children casting fishing lines in a haphazard manner.

Before long we saw Mr. Adams, his back so bent he seemed to be searching the grass for four-leaf clovers. When he got down to the dock he nodded at us, lowered himself into one of the slatted wooden chairs placed there for the comfort of hotel guests, and motioned Papa to take another one. Papa said he preferred to stand, not realizing, I guess, that the old man had trouble looking up.

Papa said, "If it's convenient, we wouldn't mind having a look at the place this evening."

Mr. Adams pulled on his lower lip for a moment. "I guess my grandson would be eager enough to show it to you. There was another chap wanted to buy the place a week or so ago, but he backed out. I'd just as soon not sell it, mind you, but young Wilfred is pestering me to get rid of it."

He told Papa that Wilf and the ladies were involved in a card game with some of the hotel guests, but would be free very soon. We could wait here for him, or meet him at the property, and he'd show us around. Papa said he'd meet him at the property. I started to object because there's no place to land a boat like this, but he waved me into silence.

The old man held up a cautionary finger. "There's only one thing about the place. The buyer must agree to leave the building on it untouched until after my soul's departed this earth."

Papa was sitting on the edge of the dock now, ready to get back into the boat. He turned a puzzled face to Mr. Adams. "That's an odd stipulation."

"What's that?"

He had to repeat himself several times before the old man could make out what he was saying.

"I know, I know," Adams said, "but there it is. Otherwise the place is not for sale."

"I'm not sure that's legal, and I'm not sure I want the place that badly," Papa enunciated.

"It's up to you."

Papa got into the boat with a skeptical roll of the eyes.

"My, that's a fine bunch of youngsters you have there." Mr. Adams struggled out of the chair and planted his cane on the dock, peering down at us as he leaned on it. I don't believe he recognized me. "You're very lucky. And they're fortunate to have a good man for a father."

"Oh, well," Papa said, embarrassed by the personal turn of the conversation, "perhaps."

"I wasn't as lucky. Mine was just plain vicious."

Papa was standing in the boat now, and kept looking out at the lake as if he'd like to make a quick getaway. Half-heartedly he said, "Surely you're exaggerating," and had to say it three times as he doesn't like to raise his voice. To us he muttered, "Whatever his father has to do with the price of tea in China!"

The old man stood for a moment in thought. "Yes, maybe I am." He paused again and said, "I tell you, at my age, it's hard to know what's real anymore and what isn't. Whether it's something I remember, or a thing told me by somebody else. Or then again, was it something I dreamt? Whatever it might be, I have a feeling in the pit of my stomach there's a reason the building can't come down. I feel strongly about that. It's cursed."

Papa took his seat, making a sound of disgust in his throat. He said to me, "Start her up, son." Under his breath, but with a smile on his face for the benefit of Mr. Adams, he said to us, "Cursed, my foot! Superstitious old fool! He'll want something exorbitant, I'll wager, for the evil spirits."

I was still holding on to the dock, wondering how much Mr. Adams could hear, afraid to look at him. "There's no-no-no place to land there, you know."

Papa said, "We can pull the boat up onshore."

"Too-too-too rocky."

He gave a deep sigh, but maintained his agreeable expression. "You always find some sort of excuse, don't you, Frederick? You always look for defeat instead of success. Some boys would say, 'I will find a way or make one,' but not our Fred, no siree." He glanced then at Mr. Adams, who smiled and nodded at the pleasantries Papa seemed to be exchanging with his son.

My arms and stomach were itching like fun, but I didn't scratch. "I've-I've-I've. We've seen Mr. Adams's property. There's no place to land a-a-a boat like this."

"There's that old tree," Harold said. I stared at him, thinking about wringing his neck.

"It'll scr-scr-scr-scratch the boat."

"We'll hold it off."

I got the engine going, muttering to myself. We waved at the old man, pushed away from the dock, and headed slowly across the lake. It would be dark soon. We had the lantern, but it wasn't really going to be of much help if I wanted to check the depth of the water. I had visions of handing the boat back over to Grandpa and Uncle Will, with the sides gouged by the tree and the propeller bent all to rat shit from running over rocks.

Bessie looked glumly at me as if she had taken on my bad mood. Nearing the other shore, I cut the engine to a crawl and nosed in toward the fallen tree where Ernie and Harold and I had gone ashore, and then cut the engine entirely. We drifted in, and they all grabbed at the tree branches while I bent over the side checking the depth. I held the boat steady, trying to keep it from getting scratched while the others clambered out onto the tree trunk. They broke off dead branches blocking their way and, giving Bessie and Tom a hand, all managed to reach dry land.

After Papa had struggled out, he asked, "Aren't you coming?"

"I'll wait," I said. "I don't-don't-don't like to leave the boat."

He stood onshore with his hands on his hips while the others trudged ahead pushing through the sumac's springy branches. "Excuses, excuses! Frederick, you never cease to amaze me. You have no sense of adventure. Aren't you even curious? You're not afraid of that so-called curse, I hope."

I shook my head. Did he really think I would admit it, if I were? He went on, "There's supposed to be some mystery of sorts concerning this place. Mr. James told me something about some nasty chap who went around murdering travelers. I forget what all he said. I'm surprised you boys haven't heard of it," he chuckled.

"We-we-we have."

He looked a little like a tire going flat. "Oh," he said. "Not a grain of truth in it, I expect."

"Th-th-there might be."

Whenever we'd heard talk of the ferryman, it had seemed more like a spooky tale than anything else, but now I wasn't sure. For one thing, there was old Mr. Adams. He did not want this place torn down. That was definite. There was something here that he didn't want dredged up. Something he'd had to run from. On the hotel veranda he'd said his father was the devil incarnate. I think that's what he'd called him. I remembered how interested he'd been in my watch. Said he'd been given one, but had given it back. It was stolen, or something.

"Come along, son, the boat will be fine."

Slowly and with great care, I tied the braided bumpers between the boat and the tree, wedged the cushions in, too, for added protection, and reluctantly followed my father as he strode with confidence up from the lake.

Someone must have taken a machete to the juniper bushes because a narrow path had been slashed through them, right up to the cabin. The door was different, too. The padlock had been removed, and the boards nailing it shut must have been taken off and then replaced because they looked loose. It wouldn't take much strength to pull them off. The others were milling about, trying to pry off the boards. One came off in Ernie's hand. "Let's pull them off and go in," Harold said. Papa was all for it and helped them pry off the boards.

"Shouldn't we wait-wait-wait for the owner?"

"Well, yes, we really should." Papa had scraped his wrist somehow and had stopped to mop at the scratch with his handkerchief.

"Too late," Harold said. The last of the boards clattered to the ground. Everyone stood around looking embarrassed about their rash attack on someone else's property.

"Why don't you push the door open?" Tom ventured from the security of his position behind Papa. Ernie gave it a gentle shove, but it didn't budge. Harold pushed it a little harder, but nothing happened.

"We'll just wait for the owners," Papa said. He glanced toward the setting sun. "I hope they come soon."

"Go get the lantern out of the boat," Harold ordered Tom.

Bessie said, "It wouldn't hurt just to peep in, would it?"

Ernie, with more enthusiasm than he'd had last time we were here, agreed. "We don't need to go in; we'll just look." He pushed hard and the door opened a crack. Tom was back with the lantern and Ernie struck a match, sheltering it with his hands while he bent over the wick to light it.

"What's that funny noise?" Bessie asked.

"Probably the owners arriving."

"No," she said. "It's coming from inside." We all listened but couldn't hear much of anything, some rustling maybe, or birds in the trees above us squeaking.

"Here goes," Harold said. He wound up and heaved his shoulder against the door with all his might. It scraped open about a foot and everyone, me included, crowded close to have a look. The air was rank with a smell I didn't recognize, foul as a closed-up outhouse, but with a different odor. It was still fairly light outside, but through the door it was black as the inside of a cow. Ernie held the lantern up. We peered into the gloom and could make out some tools hanging on a wall: tongs, an icepick, a wheelbarrow propped on its end under them.

Something flew out through the open door past our heads. Bessie shrieked and pulled Tom with her away from the door. "Wh-wh-what was that?" Papa asked, and I thought he sounded a little like me.

"I think-think-think it was a bat."

"Oh, dear God!" Papa said.

"I hate bats," Harold said and hustled away from the door.

"It's-it's-it's gone."

"I wouldn't go in there on a bet," Harold said.

Bessie said, "Oh, pooh! We're not afraid, are we, Tom?" She still had hold of his hand.

"Yes, we are," he said.

Ernie said, "I've seen enough," and handed the lantern to me. I didn't want it. I didn't even want to look in, but I guess I'm like the guy at the end of the line who gets left holding the bag.

Light from the lantern filtered through the door, turning the black interior into shades of yellow and gray. "Look!" Papa whispered behind me. He was breathing oddly, panting very quickly, as if running a race. I looked up to where he was pointing. In one corner, where the roof rafters met the walls, hung a series of short drapes, moving in waves, as if something behind them were trying to get out. In the split second it took before I realized they weren't drapes at all, I saw, in the lantern light, hundreds of shining eyes, glistening with pure, animal fear.

At one and the same moment, my father delivered a scream that lifted the hair on my neck and scalp. The colony of bats, wings rushing the air inches above our heads, fled to safety through the open door. I saw my father spin gracefully, as if he would take flight and follow them. Then his knees buckled. I caught him before he hit the stony ground and didn't even drop the lantern.

15

Sailing Over Shoals

Grandpa keeps reminding us that summer is winding down. He points out the heavy dew we get these mornings, and the mist that hangs over the lake like steam rising. He doesn't have as many chores for us, perhaps because he believes we want to spend more time with Papa. He is very generous to let us use the Bessie *boat whenever we want.*

No harm done that night, at least to the boat. Some of the rest of us fared a little worse. After my father lost consciousness, I eased him to the ground and put the lantern down. In a moment he opened his eyes, stared blankly at me, and sat up. "What's wrong?" he asked.

"You faint-faint-fainted."

"Don't be ridiculous." He got quickly to his feet, reeling, but catching his balance. He dusted off the seat of his trousers and the elbows of his suit coat, and straightened his tie. "I took a dizzy spell. Did I stumble?"

"You swooned," I said.

"Don't be absurd. Men don't swoon."

"You were fr-fr-fr scared by the bats."

He gave me a long, hard look, as if challenging me to take back what I'd said. I looked at him levelly, thinking about the truth, not saying anything, looking him in the eye the way he was always after me to do. No one else said a word. In the silence, which I thought could go on till doomsday, every other sound seemed magnified. A chipmunk crashed through the underbrush; a loon shrieked for its mate; a woodpecker hammered its beak into a nearby pine. And then we all heard a horse's hooves, wheels creaking to a halt, pinecones crunching underfoot, and, finally, voices approaching from behind the log cabin coming from the direction of the road.

In a moment we saw Wilf, propping up his bent and wizened grandfather, followed by Nora and Edna. My heart began jumping this way and that, but it was probably because of the recent exchange between me and my father. They made slow progress through the underbrush and soon stopped to let Mr. Adams catch his breath. "Sit down on this rock, Grandfather," Wilf said. He lowered the old man onto the resting place he'd discovered at a safe distance from the front of the cabin. "It would be better if you waited here. The ground's too rough; you should never have come."

"Well, I'm here, and I'll be all right in a minute," he argued. "I intend to see that nothing's disturbed."

Wilf waded through the waist-high weeds and met us at the front of the cabin. Behind him came the girls flailing at the underbrush with sticks, beating a path through. When they got close enough, my father introduced himself to Wilf, and then there were more introductions and greetings – some of them strained – and then we all stood around awkwardly not knowing what to say next. I managed to keep my back to Nora and tried to pretend she wasn't there.

"I'm afraid we jumped the gun a little," my father said, indicating the boards on the ground and the partially opened door.

"Fair enough," Wilf said, and then quietly, glancing back to where he'd left his grandfather, "You have to know what you're getting for your money. I wanted to look in myself, the other day, but I'd forgotten to bring a light."

"Do they know the building isn't part of it?" his grandfather called. "It's to remain untouched." From his position, half-hidden by the dense tangle, he couldn't see that we'd already pried open the door.

"Yes, yes, Grandfather," Wilf shouted.

I chanced a look at Nora. She seemed to be glancing in my direction, but I quickly turned my attention to Bessie, who, with the lantern, had crept up to the door and was peeping in.

"Come away, Bessie," I said.

"I'm just looking."

Tom was behind her. "Dare you to step in," he whispered.

"Don't," I said.

"Dare you."

Papa and Wilf were talking about property lines, and Ernie and Harold were talking with Nora and Edna about the dance. Ernie called out to me, "What time was it when we left the dance?"

The exact time was indelibly printed on my memory as was nearly every other detail concerning the evening. It had been a quarter after ten. To avoid looking at anyone, I searched the evening sky for the answer and said, "I don't remember."

When I looked back at the doorway of the cabin, Tom was holding up the lantern as high as he could and Bessie was nowhere in sight. I stepped quickly to the door in time to see her picking her way gingerly across the filthy floor. At the same moment there was a spongy crunch of rotten wood giving way, and she sat down suddenly with a yelp. "Godfathers!" she screeched. "I went right through!"

The others crowded around the door to look, shoving the door open farther. "Help me!" she yelped. She tried to stand up, but her foot slipped and she sat down again with her legs dangling into the crawl space under the cabin. Everybody began offering advice all at the same time. "Shove a ladder in for her," Harold said, as if a ladder would miraculously appear out of the darkening night. "Creep out on your stomach," Ernie called to her.

"No! It's too slimy."

The floor was carpeted with a combination of bat dung and moss and what looked like old sawdust. She tried again to stand up, but another piece of the floor gave way.

"What's all the fuss about?" old Mr. Adams kept calling, but no one answered him. He was struggling to get up, but the rock on which he was seated was too low. "You're not opening the place up, are you?" he shouted.

Nora started back toward him. "No, no," she shouted. "The little girl has got herself in a pickle of some sort and wants to be rescued."

"Eh?" he said.

I turned my attention back to the cabin. Ernie was saying, "Someone will have to go in after her. Tom's the lightest."

Tom shrank back against me and looked up in horror to see if I was agreeing with Ernie. "I'll go in," I said.

Ernie looked relieved and said, "If you keep close to the edges, the floor might hold."

Harold said, "Doubt it. You'll go through for sure."

Father, looking pale and defeated, massaged his forehead with the tips of his fingers and for once didn't have an opinion.

Wilf said, "Even if he does go through, he's unlikely to hurt himself. There can't be much depth there. That crawl space won't be more than three or four feet deep."

Meanwhile Bessie was saying in a small voice, "I think I'm going to burst into tears any minute."

"Don't cry, Bessie," Tom called. His voice was small and tight as if he might burst into tears any minute, himself. He cleared his throat. "Be a brave little soldier."

Edna moved closer to the door to offer words of comfort to Bessie. She put a handkerchief over her nose to block the rank odor. I slipped in past her and stood for a moment to see if the floor would take my weight. "Ernie, hold the lantern up higher!" I called. Close to one wall, I moved warily along the floor, greasy with dung. I could feel it give slightly underfoot, but so far, it remained intact. I inched closer to Bessie, who was stretching her hands out as far as she could to reach mine, but our arms weren't quite long enough. I shuffled my feet a little closer to her, grasped one hand, then the other, and half lifted, half dragged her over to me. "Go along close to the wall," I said. She eased around me and scooted out. Everyone outside cheered except for poor Mr. Adams, who kept demanding to know what was going on. "The little girl's been rescued," Nora shouted at him. "She was trapped, but her brother got her out."

"What did you say?"

I turned to retrace my steps back to the door. "I need more light," I called to Ernie and, in a moment, he thrust the lantern in on the crook of a tree branch. I reached out to touch the wall for support. Quickly, I jerked my hand back to rub off on the seat of my trousers whatever furry slime I'd just contacted. That's when my foot skidded sideways in the muck. In the next second a large section of floor collapsed with a whining crunch, and I dropped a jarring but short distance, landing on my stomach in the rubble under the cabin. For a moment I had the breath knocked out of me and wasn't aware of anything but the gasping pulling-in sound in the back of my throat as I tried to get air back into my chest. I could hear my father saying, "Oh dear God!" over and over as if he were about to pray, but couldn't get started. "Frederick," he called, panic-stricken, "Frederick, are you all right?"

"I'm not hurt," I was finally able to call back.

Bessie was wailing, "Freddie! Freddie! I'm sorry! It was all Tom's fault!"

"I'm all right," I called. My voice sounded muffled because I'd gone right down flat into the crawl space. I reached out with my hands to try to get an idea of what I'd landed on that was so hard and bumpy. It felt like one of the balls you use for carpet bowls.

Up above I could hear various people offering advice, Harold still going on about a ladder, and Tom arguing, "It was not my fault!" And Bessie, still wailing, "Yes it was! You dared me!"

Ernie must have managed to shove the lantern closer to where I'd gone through the floor. In its glow from above I saw that the part of the floor that had fallen in was actually a trapdoor whose hinges had rusted away. Beneath it, I was able to make out a round stone and sticks with the bark peeled off, and then I noticed that the round stone was grinning at me with a row of teeth. The shriek that came out of me tore my throat.

Outside, it was like an echo of shrieks and, above it, my father shouting, "What's wrong, what's wrong?"

I scrambled to my feet, covering my face in horror. I'd landed on the bony remains of a dead body.

The floor came to just below the level of my armpits. Quickly I pressed the flat of my hands down on it to hoist myself up, but again pieces of it broke off, and again I went down to find myself crouched over the fleshless face of God knows who. One of the ferryman's victims, possibly, because what else could these bones be? Grandpa's story was true! I scrambled up and tried to make my escape, and again the floor gave way like a sheet of rotten river ice. "I don't think I can get out," I called hoarsely.

I was shaking like someone with the plague, and felt myself, and heard myself, retching – over and over – but nothing came up. Oddly, I didn't feel like some poor moron with weak nerves; it was more like waking up from a nightmare and starting to think, thank God it was only a nightmare, and then being hit with the realization that it was your worst fears come true.

This was real.

There was silence, now, outside the doorway. In a moment I heard Wilf ask in a loud whisper, "What's down there?"

It took me a moment to clear my throat. "A corpse."

"How the devil did it get there?"

"Better take-take-take the old man back home. And the girls," I added. I could hear whispers from outside and was aware of shuffling and movement. In the lantern light I looked around at all the bones. There may have been the remains of more than one body down here. Something glinted near my foot, and I moved it gently with the toe of my boot. When I saw what it was, I stopped breathing for a moment and then quickly kicked dirt over it.

I put all my strength into trying to hoist myself up again closer to the wall and, after a couple of tries, made it to a standing position and finally crept out. In the clear night air I staggered and had to lean against a tree to get my balance. My father touched my shoulder – a pat, not a slap – and I took several deep breaths to get my mind working again. I could scarcely believe what I'd seen. I could scarcely bear to think what I was thinking.

Bessie leaned her head close to my ribs. I was going to stroke her hair to let her know I wasn't angry with her, but I thought better of it. She would have chewed me out for mucking it up with my filthy hands.

Ernie and Harold stood in the doorway holding the lantern high, peering into the hole in the floor. They both let out a whistle. "It's a skeleton all right," Ernie said.

Papa glanced in and quickly backed away. "We'll have to go to the police."

It only took me a second to see how wrong that would be. How cruel. "No, don't," I said.

He swung around. "Pardon?"

"Don't tell the police."

I could see a frown deepen on his face. "Clearly a crime has been committed. The police have to be notified."

This was more than simply letting sleeping dogs lie. I had a half-formed picture in my mind of a boy hiding, peering out from behind something, perhaps catching sight of his father as he whacked some innocent traveler over the head with a blunt object, a shovel maybe, or a crowbar, until the victim fell down dead and bleeding. Perhaps he saw him take what coins and possessions he could find. A watch. Perhaps his father threw it to him, said, "Take it, it's yours now," and then stuffed the corpse under the floor of a log building. The son would see him go about his business as if nothing had happened, see him wipe sweat off his brow, grin, tell him to get out if he couldn't take it, tell him not to be so soft. Perhaps the boy's loathing and anger would eventually get the better of him. It was possible that Grandpa knew only part of the story.

Wilf had taken his grandfather and the girls back. I was trying to wrap my arms around myself and rub them at the same time to make myself stop shivering. Tom and Bessie had joined the boys trying to get a glimpse of the skeleton. Bessie pushed her way between them with her hands up over her eyes, but with her fingers spread. "Don't look, Tom," she said. "You won't be able to take it. It's too grillsome for words."

Papa said, "We'll go over and use the phone at the hotel."

"No need. It-it-it hap-hap-happened a long time ago."

"A crime is a crime," he said. "If you came home after a holiday and found that someone had robbed you, would you neglect to notify the police simply because it happened some time prior to your arrival on the scene of the crime? I think I know my civic duty."

I could see that I was going to have to spell out for him why we should just leave well enough alone, that if he involved the police, the whole thing would become public. The newspapers would take it up, and soon Mr. Adams would be asked a multitude of questions about what he remembers, and the end of his life would be just about as painful as its beginning. Perhaps more so. It took a while, but with Ernie's help and Harold's, we told him everything Grandpa had told us about the evil ferryman and his probable connection to old Mr. Adams.

"It's all surmise," he said. "You've built something on rumors and tall tales. I still think we should let the police investigate. Let them decide what to do."

Sometimes there has to be an end point, I was thinking. You can't go on forever letting the circumstances of your life push you around. The old man had been victim to a waking nightmare long enough. I said, "We're not telling anyone."

My father shot me a stern glance. "I beg your pardon?"

Maybe he couldn't make out what I'd said because I hadn't stuttered. I said it louder. "Don't tell!"

He stared at me for a moment. "That was childish!" he said. "And so we'll simply ignore it. I would like you all to come along now and get into the boat. My conscience would not allow me to rest if I didn't report such an obvious crime."

"Come along," he repeated, heading down to the boat. The others moved reluctantly away from the door. Tom and Bessie began slowly to follow him. Harold shrugged and went along, too. I took the lantern from Ernie and stayed where I was. My heart drummed inside me and I could scarcely breathe. I tensed my muscles waiting for some unseen punishment to flatten me.

Ernie looked perplexed. He was standing halfway between me and our father. Papa turned and said, "Frederick, I'm quite prepared to paddle the boat across the lake myself, you know, since you have decided to be so infantile about this." We stood facing each other for another moment, stubborn as stones, a space like miles between us. He turned then, and strode as best he could, given the rough terrain, to the boat.

Stubborn as stones, I thought, and saw myself as a great square block of granite and him as something else, limestone maybe, related but different. "Father!" I called.

He stopped and turned. I'd never called him Father before, always Papa. I felt taller, bulkier, and straightened my back to fill out this newfound space. There was no sound, anywhere. "I n-n-n-need help putting the boards back."

Silence.

I rummaged around holding the lantern in front of me until I'd located the boards. I put the lantern down and attempted to hold a large board and, at the same time, hammer it back into place with a rock. After a long pause, Ernie began to help, and then Tom came back and handed up boards. No one spoke. Harold stood in the path, and Bessie watched anxiously as our father made his way alone to the boat.

Wilf had removed the padlock. I'd go to him tomorrow and get him to put it back on. The bones wouldn't be any the deader for having to wait another few years. Time enough for truth to be discovered. We finished the job as best we could.

Father was sitting in the back of the boat, arms folded across his chest, chin raised, staring into the dead branches of the capsized tree. I looked at him in his defeat, and felt like a murderer myself. We were all pretty quiet. Ernie was cracking his knuckles. Harold kept his trap shut and held the lantern while I got the engine going. He helped Tom and Bessie in.

"Shall I sit with you, Papa?" Bessie said in her kindest voice.

"Whatever you like," he said, his own voice flat, echoing in the stillness of the night.

Ernie and Harold pushed us off and we were soon underway with the stars guiding us back to Sunnybank. If there were any shoals, we were sailing right on over them.

"Little Sir Echo, how do you do? Hello . . ." Bessie sang quietly.

"Hello . . ." I answered, quietly, seriously.

16

Change

After breakfast we carried water for the cottage folks to do the washing and replaced a few weak boards in the dock, at Grandpa's request, until we heard the little yacht that goes up the lake twice a week with corn, tomatoes, onions, peaches, etc., blowing for Mr. Ash's cottage. So Ernie and Harold and I put the sail into the boat and quickly rowed there for some corn. It is a mile to Mr. Ash's and was good exercise for us. We also got two dozen eggs and put the sail up and sailed home. We then ate apples and plums and worked hard at nothing until dinner. After dinner I took my father up the lake in the Bessie *boat as he had some business to attend to.*

Uncle Will had supplied us with two containers of gasoline to make sure we would not run out. With a funnel, I poured some of it into the engine's small tank. Auntie Lizzie had thought we all seemed unusually preoccupied during the morning and needed some sun and exercise to liven us up. "You should be making the most of the last warm days of August," she told us. Everyone else piled into the *Jumbo* and rowed to the bathing place for an afternoon of swimming, so my father and I had the *Bessie* boat to ourselves.

"Shall I untie, Frederick?"

"Yes, please, Father." We were speaking very formally and politely to each other after our difference of opinion the night before. We sat side by side in the front of the boat. As we cut along smoothly up the lake, he stared with intense interest at the south shore, and I saw a lot to fascinate me along the north shore. At one point we said, at the same time, "The trees are starting to change." We both came close to smiling.

As we neared Rideau Ferry, we saw a young man in a canoe pulling away from the dock. I recognized him instantly: Nora's beau. He didn't give us a glance, but squinted into the sun and dipped deep with his paddle, his shoulder muscles bulging. We tied the boat and walked slowly up to the hotel. Edna was reading in the front lobby. She said to my father, "I guess you'll want to talk to Wilf."

"If I may, or else Mr. Adams."

"He's not very well today, I'm afraid. I'll get Wilf."

We stood in the spacious hall facing a wide staircase. Sun streamed in through large screened windows in the dining room to the left and in a small sitting room to the right of the lobby. There was no one about, although we could hear a clatter of dishes coming from the dining room. When Wilf came down the stairs, he looked as though he had slept poorly, eyes hollow, face lined. "Have you come about the property, Mr. Dickinson?" he said to Father.

My father cleared his throat. "Well, yes, I have. Under the present circumstances, though, I . . . it . . . would seem inappropriate to. . . ."

"You're quite right. It's out of the question." Wilf said. "The last thing I want is publicity – for Grandfather's sake. I owe him that much. He's always been good to me, providing for me after my father died, giving me a home, although I've caused him a few problems over the years. I suppose I've been aware of something black blotting his past, but I've never really believed it. Until last night. So, the place cannot be sold at this time, welcome as the money might be. I have, in fact, replaced the padlock."

He paused, choosing his words, sizing up Father. "I don't suppose I have any right to ask this, but would it be possible for you and your children to keep this incident to yourselves? At least for now?"

"I don't see how . . . that is . . . it's not a question of. . . ." I looked my father fully in the face. "Yes, of course," he murmured, frowning, looking away. I could tell he was wrestling with his conscience, wrestling with his own rules about duty and justice and child rearing. I knew how things looked to him – either black or white – no shades in between. What he was being asked to do was deeply shrouded in black.

We all stood around awkwardly studying the floor for a moment. "Could-could-could I just say good-bye to your grandfather?" I asked. Summer was nearly over. We would soon all go our separate ways, back to the orderly world of autumn followed by winter and then spring. Old Mr. Adams belonged to summer haze, and campfire smoke, and wind and thunder and lightning. And to sweet dreams that don't come true. And bad ones that do. Perhaps I had an idea of assuring him his secret was safe with me.

"I don't see why not," Wilf said. "He's not quite himself though, I should warn you. The nightmares have been replaced by something else. Although, as it turns out, they weren't just nightmares. I don't know whether we'll ever know the true story."

He led us up the stairs to a large bedroom in which the curtains were drawn to keep out the full strength of the sun. On a high square bed, the old man lay propped against pillows, eyes closed, hands folded on top of the white counterpane. His sparse hair was neatly combed and his mustache trimmed. Beside him in an armchair sat Nora, her legs curled up under her, resting her head on her hand. She had never looked more beautiful.

She got up when we came in, greeted us politely, then

leaned over the old man to tell him he had visitors. He opened his eyes and she smiled at us briefly, sadly, and slipped out of the room. I could not resist staring after her.

Father shook hands with him, and I forced my attention back to Mr. Adams. He looked at me in surprise. "Willie!" he said. "You've come home at last. Has school finished, then? They haven't thrown you out have they, lad? Haha!"

I didn't know how to reply. He had taken my hand and was pulling me close to embrace me. Awkwardly, I submitted and looked at Wilf for guidance. He shrugged. "He thinks you're his son. Willie was my father."

He shouted, "It isn't Willie, Grandfather. It's a boy from down the lake." Wilf looked at me. "Fred, is it?" I nodded. "His name's Fred," he shouted.

Mr. Adams still had me by the hand, was still looking at me fondly, ignoring Wilf. "Ah, yes, my boy, my boy. Why, my soul and body, look at you! You're next thing to a man! Where has the time gone? Open those drapes," he said to Wilf, "till we get a better look at him. Isn't he like his mother?" I sensed my father moving closer to me.

Wilf threw the curtains wide and we were awash in sunshine, bleached pale as ghosts. The old man drew me closer and touched my face, turning it to the side. "Well, he's his own man, isn't he? You can see the strength right in his face." He chuckled to himself and said to my father, "I'm not half proud of the boy, am I?"

Father was beside me now, nodding politely.

In a low voice Wilf said, "I'm afraid last night was too much for him. I'm not sure whether he knew what was going on or not, but by the time we got him home he was raving. It's as though he's escaped into some other time in his life."

Mr. Adams was speaking to Father, "I have a poor head for names, but I rarely forget a face. I know I know you. You'll have to forgive me."

"Dickinson," Father said, actually raising his voice this time.

"The very name I was searching for," Mr. Adams said.

"And this is my eldest son, Frederick . . . Fred," he shouted. His voice had taken on a bit of a quaver I wasn't used to hearing, but it may have been because he wasn't used to raising his voice.

"The apple of your eye," Mr. Adams said, hiking himself higher on the pillows, back in present time for the moment. "You can just see it the way you look at him." He smiled at Father, and his wrinkled face seemed as fragile as cracked china.

Father wasn't looking at me, but down at his own inter-laced fingers, twisting them hard enough to crack the knuckles. Mr. Adams was still talking. "Yes, siree, you can always spot the fond papa." Father barely raised his head. But when, for one brief moment, he glanced at me, I thought he had something in his eye, because he blinked a couple of times. It may have been only the sun. In any case, I looked away quickly.

"I don't blame you one bit," Mr. Adams said. "They're awful good, these lads, aren't they?" He seemed to be in both the present and the past. "I expect you're just as proud of your son as I am of mine."

Father was nodding and swallowing hard.

"Eh?"

"Yes, I am."

"What's that?"

"Yes," Father shouted. "I am proud of him."

Our eyes met for a brief flicker. He was pressing his lips together hard against his teeth the way I do myself, sometimes, to keep from getting too emotional.

After a moment he said, "We'll say good-bye now, so as not to tire you."

"What's that?"

Wilf shouted, "They have to leave. They're saying good-bye."

"Nice of you to come, lads. Is it getting late? I can't think where I've left my watch."

I could. A shudder ran through me.

Father shook hands with him and then turned to leave. I reached out to shake hands, too. The old man held my hand and smiled warmly. "Ah, my boy, it's wonderful to have you back. Does your mother know you're home?"

I smiled at him and patted his arm as I released my hand. "I'll let her know," I said.

Downstairs we could hear women's voices chattering in the

sitting room, but saw no sign of either Edna or Nora. We left quietly, and in silence made our way back down to the boat. I stood with the bow rope in my hand, waiting for Father to untie the stern. I looked back across the lawn and up at the hotel with its carved gables and peaceful veranda, and saw Nora leaning wistfully against a pillar. I stared at her briefly and turned away.

Father held the boat while I started the engine. "Any other prop-prop-properties you want to look at?" I regretted my words as soon as I'd said them. Ernie would have said, *Sarcasm will get you nowhere*, but I wasn't being sarcastic. I had no conversational ideas in my head and just blurted out the first thing that popped in.

I looked up from the engine to glimpse his expression, but he was taking my words at face value. "I haven't the heart for it. Never did have, really, I guess. I thought, you know . . . I thought, at the time, having our own cottage by the lake would bring us closer . . . bring me closer . . . what I mean is, to you boys, and Bessie."

I wasn't used to my father saying what was on his mind like this. If Ernie were here, he'd have gone and sat in the backseat of the boat.

He said, "I miss you youngsters when you go off to the lake, you know." This surprised me. I remembered, sheepishly, how skeptical I'd been of Grandma's thoughts on the subject. He went on, "Time's moving too fast for me, Fred. You've begun to grow up. You know I hate excuses, but, well . . . it's been hard, son, I don't mind telling you, it's been awfully hard since your mother died. I've grown hard myself, I guess, set in my ways. I'm afraid I've put a fence between us, somehow. And now, you know, now, before it's too late I. . . ."

There was a long silence while I waited for him to go on, but he didn't. "I know," I said. He got in and we pushed off.

Puffs of cloud floated above, drifting together, taking on new shapes against the brilliant blue of the sky. It was a fine day. Small waves slapped at the bow as I steered a course parallel to the bridge to watch a motorcar rattle over it, shaking the bridge, peeling off at the other end, wheeling down the road in a cloud of dust. It was the first one we'd seen in the area, and I felt very modern and excited just watching it. They're the coming thing, although Grandpa maintains they'll never replace the trusty horse and carriage.

"Perhaps I should remarry," Father said.

I could feel his eyes on me, waiting for a reply, a comment, any kind of acknowledgment that I had understood what he'd just said.

"Re-re-re-marry?" My voice sounded tinny this close to the bridge. I turned the *Bessie* and headed back down the lake, squinting straight ahead in the sunlight. I couldn't look him in the eye because I was thinking about my mother.

"Maybe we need to make some changes in our lives. I'm not saying it will happen, it's just something I've been thinking about."

Ernie hates change. If he'd been here he would have jumped right out of the boat and swum home. I was considering Tom and Bessie now, especially Bessie. They'd improve with a bit of mothering, no doubt. Ernie and I, well, we could probably take it. We could take anything. But I didn't want ever to forget our mother and I was afraid it was already happening. I searched my mind for the sound of her voice.

Quietly, Father said, "No one ever knows what it's like to be inside someone else's life." He was looking down at the floor of the boat as if what he'd said was something to be ashamed of. He said, "Our lives are like a game of charades. Guess why I'm acting this way, is what we seem to say."

I looked away, but nodded. He was probably right.

I had a sudden picture of my mother, something I didn't even know I'd remembered. It had nothing to do with me or him or any of us. I must have been in the kitchen doorway, alone, taking mental notes without even knowing I was. She was absorbed in what she was doing, leaning over the cooking stove with its lids off, black circles propped against each other on top of the range, and the fire inside, two red-hot wells. In one hand she wielded a cone of burning paper and, in the other – holding it high above her head – a freshly plucked and cleaned chicken. Flames licked at the remains of its pinfeathers, singeing them off. The chicken writhed and spiraled with every graceful twist of her wrist. Yellow flames from the cone winked and flirted, then rushed at the pale bird, engulfing it on all sides. And she didn't so much as flinch. It was like a secret rite or, maybe, a feat of magic. At the time I thought, she can do *anything*.

I smelled the burnt feathers. I saw the perspiration running down her reddened cheeks, damp straggles of hair clinging to her neck in curls. It was not a picture you'd see in a photograph album.

"I relied on your mother so much," Father said quietly.

Maybe he gained strength from her, and then lost it when she died. Maybe I had, too. She had been real, not just wishful thinking. Aloud, I said, "I know."

He glanced at me and away and I said, "We-we-we-could all take a change or two."

He folded his arms across his chest, leaning against the seat back, stretching his legs straight out under the deck. I think he was heaving a huge sigh, but it was hard to hear over the put-put-put of the engine.

17

Moving Forward

Yesterday was our last full day at the cottage. We had to stand in the kitchen doorway while Auntie Lizzie measured us with a yardstick and marked our height. Harold has hardly grown at all; I've grown two inches and a half; Ernie almost the same; and Tom and Bessie an inch each. Ettie is taller than all of us, but claims she has stopped growing for which she is thankful. We were then told to go and polish our boots for going back to Perth to Grandma's. We did a lot of chores in the afternoon, stocking the woodpile for next summer, folding the hammocks and putting them away. We got the shutters out from under the cottage all ready to nail up over the windows just before we leave. We pulled the Jumbo up onto dry

*land and turned it over and stashed the oars, mast,
and fishing rods above the boathouse rafters.*

*After supper we invited everyone down to our
camp, and Auntie Min made a lot of taffy and
cream candy, and we had a magnificent time
eating it and hearing stories. After that we lit the
lantern, and Harold and Ernie and I played
FLINCH in the tent until ten o'clock. We then
roasted some apples on the top of the lamp
chimney (our lantern is a candle with a lamp
chimney over it and is so arranged as to be
carried by a handle) and ate them.*

It was terrifically cold during the night, with a heavy dew covering the outside of our tent. We could see our breath when
we got up, but the sun soon began to do its duty and it was
warm by nine o'clock. Father left early in the morning,
procuring a ride with Mr. Ash as far as the Smiths Falls
railway station. I walked as far as Mr. Ash's with him. On the
way I told him as politely as I could that I didn't want to sew
robes for a living. He started to frown, but, on the whole,
didn't seem badly upset. "Well," he said, "in that case, we'll
just have to think of something more suitable." We shook
hands, and then he got up into Mr. Ash's wagon.

How civilized, I thought.

After breakfast, which was kindly provided for us by the
cottage folk, we set to work to dismantle Beaver Camp. We

took apart our bed, shaking out the blankets and folding them, packed up our dishes and pots in a crate, and returned them to the cottage along with our supplies. A mouse had had himself a feast in our oatmeal, which we didn't notice until Ettie spotted a trail of it leading up to the cottage, where it had leaked out through a hole in the bag.

"Why didn't you store that in a tin?" Auntie Lizzie scolded.

We had, but then we needed the tin for storing worms for fishing. We didn't bother to explain because she was going at the floors of the cottage with a broom so fiercely, we were in danger of having our shins cracked.

"You can just take it right out again," she said. "I won't have mouse-riddled oatmeal inside this cottage."

Grandpa had escaped to the safety of the out-of-doors and a cedar bench he'd made for himself earlier in the summer, where he sat filling his pipe for his last smoke of the summer. "Dump it out by the woodpile," he said. "Give the chipmunks a corking good picnic for a change."

Uncle Will had hitched up Nellie and come out to the lake to pick up the luggage and any passengers willing to forego the last *Bessie* ride of the summer. Grandpa said he'd make the big sacrifice, and Auntie Min said, "You go in the boat, Lizzie. You're a stronger swimmer than I am." And Auntie Lizzie said, "As far as I know, we're not being asked to swim behind the boat, Min." And Auntie Min said, "But, what would Father do without me on the way back?" And Grandpa said behind his hand, "Smoke."

Uncle Will said to me, "How would you like to ferry the rest of them up to Perth?" And Harold yelled, "No fair!" and rammed his fist into the side of the buggy, making Nellie jump sideways. And Uncle Will gave him a stern look.

By three o'clock in the afternoon we were all dressed in our best clothes ready to load the remainder of our gear into the boat to go back to Perth. Uncle Will, Auntie Min, and Grandpa had already left. Bessie and Tom were going around saying good-bye to their favorite trees and to two or three large rocks they were particularly fond of.

When we managed to get everyone into the boat, Ettie said, "Let's go for a spin to say good-bye to the lake, couldn't we?" She was looking at me and I was going to look at Auntie Lizzie, but then I remembered I was captain of the boat, at least for the occasion, and said, "Certainly, my dear."

She gave me a pained glare. "Don't let it go to your head, sunshine." Boat captains should never be obliged to transport their cousins for any great distance.

The lake had taken on the seedy look it gets at the end of summer, green with algae. A haze hung over it making everything in the distance indistinct, as if we were only imagining shoreline trees, the drowned lands, the bathing beach. The sun warmed us, but didn't burn. Here and there along the shore we pointed out maples to each other – bits of them spattered red – and the odd birch gleaming in the sun, flashing a few gold leaves like a scatter of coins, a preview of the glorious color to come.

We went as far as Rideau Ferry and circled around just before the bridge. Ours was almost the only boat. Across the lake someone paddled a canoe, but the fishermen and cottagers had all left the lake, or were getting ready to leave. Up on the bridge, the bridge master cast out a fishing line, and then reeled it slowly in. I wondered how he kept himself occupied once winter set in.

Tom and Bessie were in the front seat beside me. "If we had a motor car, we'd be home in jig time," Tom said.

"What's the rush?" I said. "In a boat, you have time-time-time to think." What I meant was, you don't feel as if your life is getting beyond itself when you're in a boat. You feel in control.

Ettie said her good-byes to Rideau Ferry and to the bridge, and then we nipped along the far shore past the old Oliver place cowering above its grisly secrets. We all had our necks in a knot staring back at it, but even it had faded in the afternoon haze. Like a memory. It seems to me that the bare facts of a thing cling to the edges of your mind forever. But feelings don't. There's a whole big empty cave in there that swallows up the hair rising on your arms or your stomach threatening to rebel. Or the way you felt about a girl. Just as well, too, or you'd be stuck in the past forever. I took out my watch and glanced at it. I waited until the large hand jerked toward the next minute, and then put it back in my pocket, satisfied that this was the way of the world. We move forward.

We were catching up to the canoe. I was surprised to

recognize Nora's beau paddling it as if he didn't care whether he got where he was going or not. In front of him, surrounded by cushions, lolled a girl, leaning her head back against his chest, looking up into his eyes, and he was smiling down into hers. The whole scene could have been quite romantic, but it wasn't. He bent over to kiss the girl, and then straightened when he noticed how close our boat was.

I looked back to see Auntie Lizzie raise her eyebrows and look the other way. The rest of us gawked like owls. I thought Ettie's jaw would fall right off the bottom of her face. The girl definitely was not Nora. Bessie called out to Ettie in her shrillest voice, "Say, isn't that Nora's beau cuddling with someone else?"

Ettie put her finger up to her lips. Bessie didn't seem to realize voices carry when you have to yell above the sound of an engine. "Well, isn't it?" she insisted. I could have clapped my hand over her mouth, but I didn't. Good enough for him, I thought. I began thinking up speeches like, *The cad! Little did she know when she spurned me! I would never have been a two-timer!* And then a quiet but annoying voice broke in with, *You were never actually in the running, buster.*

We swished past them and I looked back to see how they were taking the swells from our boat. At eight miles an hour, we didn't do much damage. They were rocking like babes in a cradle.

We headed back across the lake and took one last turn past Sunnybank. With the shutters up it seemed to have its eyes closed, hibernating until next summer. "Good-bye, Sunnybank!" Bessie called. Tom was going to yell, "Good-bye," too, but he looked at me and back at Ernie and Harold, and we all had our jaws set in a manly way. At least mine was because I was trying not to feel emotional about leaving, about the end of summer, about not ever being able to have that particular summer back again. Even the miserable parts.

I turned the boat toward the inlet leading into the first lock and cut back on the throttle. The gates were open, but Mr. Buchanan was beginning to wheel them closed. When he saw us he stopped, and through his megaphone called for us to come ahead. He had just opened for a boat ahead of us. I was concentrating on getting between the enormous gates and not paying much attention to the other boat. Mr. Buchanan was signaling for it to move ahead to make room for us. I edged our boat next to the high stone wall behind it, and Harold and Ernie grabbed at the chains hanging down to keep us from drifting. I cut the engine.

The boat ahead of us was a longer, wider version of our own, with wicker chairs in back instead of bench seats. Sitting in them were Nora, her sister, Edna, and a woman who was probably their mother. I hate when things like this happen. Ettie was already in a conversation with the girls. Wilf, captain of their boat, tipped his hat. Beside him, his grandfather appeared to have shrunk, half-hidden as he was by cushions and a knit shawl.

It doesn't take very long to get a boat through the locks. It seems like seconds if you're occupied helping out the lockmaster, as we've done on occasion. It takes ten minutes, if you're in a boat on a good day. If you're stuck in a boat in a lock and the boat closest to you is filled with a girl you've made an ass of yourself over all summer, it seems like a life sentence. I wondered if she'd caught sight of her two-timing gent in the canoe. We'd probably hear soon enough with Bessie on board.

The gates were closed and the water was rushing in through the sluice gates, raising us up to the first level. The higher we rose, the more I felt like a sunken log. I kept trying not to look at her, but I caught her glancing at me a couple of times. I managed to keep busy bending over the engine with an oily rag. When I got tired of that, I made a neat coil out of our mooring ropes on the bow deck, and then stared down between the boat and the stone wall to watch the water seethe and eddy as it nudged us upward. The Maberly girls were inviting Ettie to visit them at their home in Ottawa.

Mr. Buchanan called down to us, "There'll be a wee wait 'fore we lock you through. The *Jopl's* stuck in the upper lock with engine trouble. Mought's well stretch your legs for the duration."

Once out of the lock, Ernie paddled us in to the wharf behind Wilf's boat. We fellows scrambled out to tie up. "Want to hi-hi-hike up to the upper lock?" I said to them. It was a chance to see our friends on the *Jopl* one last time this summer and a chance to leave all the ladies behind to chatter and mind the boat.

I lagged behind just long enough to tip my cap to old Mr. Adams, hoping he'd remember me and not think I was someone else from some other era. He squinted up at me. "What's that, boy?"

"G'day to you, sir."

"Very fine," he said, "very fine."

I took off then without so much as a glance at the Maberly girls. Ernie and Harold and Tom had gone on ahead. Trudging along, I heard Mr. Adams say to Wilf, "Isn't that the lad that's so stuck on our Nora?"

I cringed and picked up the pace. My fame knew no bounds, apparently. Nora must have told him, too. I imagined him wheezing and chuckling heartily over my naked, but public, swan dive. My ears felt scalded. I could hear hurried footsteps on the grassy path behind me, but decided not to glance back.

"Fred," she called. I slowed and threw her a quick look over my shoulder. "Wait up a bit, can't you?"

I stopped and turned. Arms folded, I scowled at Nora from under the brim of my cap. She looked as beautiful as ever, her hair undone, flying about her face. She was hauling at the skirt of her dress to keep from tripping as she hurried to catch up to me. I caught sight of her slender ankles and scuffed shoes, and it occurred to me that we men are the luckier of the sexes. I couldn't imagine being tripped up by layers and folds of cloth every time I took a notion to break into a run. I guess ladies are never expected to run.

"I'm sorry," she said, out of breath.

She was apologizing! I was stunned into staring at her. I pushed my cap back and scratched my head because it never occurred to me that she would actually apologize for all the embarrassment she'd caused me. I didn't know what to say so I said, "Well, thanks for a-a-a-p-p-pologizing, anyway." I put my hands in my pockets and looked at the ground. I wouldn't have minded if she'd let the whole incident rest.

"Pardon? Apologizing for what?"

I looked blankly back at her looking blankly at me. "For-for-for . . ." My eyes felt round as doorknobs and my Adam's apple was fighting with my collar and tie as I tried to swallow.

She interrupted, "I only meant to say, sorry for running after you. I guess you want to catch up to the other boys."

Right. No apology. I registered the words "other boys" and saw how I must look to her. A kid. Bony big wrists dangling too long for my coat sleeves, and my pant legs barely reaching the tops of my boots. "It's all r-r-r-right," I said. My voice sounded rusty, as if it might quit altogether.

"I just want to ask you why you seem so angry with me?"

I felt my eyes blinking at her. "I-I-I-I."

She slipped her arm through mine and said, "I'll walk with you up to the next lock and you can tell me what's wrong."

Her arm felt heavy, clutching, unlike my first experience strolling up to the store with her to buy sodas. The heat of

her body so close to mine made me dizzy. She smelled like . . .
cut flowers, I was thinking, but . . . maybe flowers that have
been in the house too long would be more accurate. It seemed
like miles between the two locks. I was taking long strides to
get there, and Nora was bounding along like a jackrabbit to
keep up.

"Stop," she said. She sounded out of breath. I came
smartly to a halt. "One of these days, I shall wear nothing but
trousers and stout boots, and I'll cut my corsets to shreds."

I guess my mouth was hanging open.

"Do I shock you?"

I shook my head, no. She threw back hers and laughed . . .
at my blazing ears, I expect.

She said, "Why should men have all the fun? I'd jolly well
like to go tramping around wearing whatever I like." She
grinned mischievously. "Or nothing at all, like some people I
know."

She saw me wince and said teasingly, "Oh, now, don't be
such a delicate little goose. I don't think anyone was injured
by that performance of yours."

"I was," I said, quietly.

She looked into my eyes, her own all round and serious.
"Why ever for?"

"You-you-you told your beau. And quite a few others," I
added.

"Oh, piffle! Who will remember in a year? Or even in a
month? Anyway, I have no beau. The scoundrel!" She turned

her head to hide the hurt look that had come into her eyes. When she turned back she said, "I've been feeling pretty low for the way he jilted me, but I got over him. Men don't care a fig about feelings. They just do anything they like, while women have to sit there and take it."

I had stopped being aware of the heat and the way she smelled, and the way she made me feel all excited and jumpy. I stood where I was, stroking my upper lip, checking for bristles, studying her. "That's not true. Some-some-some men care more about feelings than-than-than some women." She stood back from me and gave me a kind of sidelong look as though she was only seeing me for the first time.

"Really! You're beginning to sound like my mother. I suppose you mean me."

Little warning noises like popcorn popping were going on inside me and I thought, this conversation is a loaded gun. Her eyes were turning rock hard. Talking about emotional things with women is not for the fainthearted, I thought, and stored that away for Ernie's future edification. And Tom's.

"Do you?" she repeated.

"Not-not-not really." She was glaring at me, waiting for me to go on, either to incriminate myself, or to tell her what she wanted to hear. "B-b-but, you might p-p-put yourself in-in-in my place, for once."

She frowned at me. I wanted to tell her you have to imagine you're the other person for a minute or two to find out how fragile their feelings are. But I didn't. Even if I could have blurted it out, I don't think she'd have got it. So we just stood there, me rubbing my chin now, and the lower edge of my jaw, hoping for stubble; and Nora, sizing me up, trying to figure out how in the world she could possibly put herself in my place.

"You men are all alike," she said, "impossible to understand."

I shrugged as if I was kind of agreeing with her and kind of not, looking for the safest course. But I had to smile. *You men*, I was thinking. I liked that, me and all the other men. I'm not a total outcast; I'm like the others, hard to understand. Like the surface of the lake, there's more to me than what you see.

I made a move to go up along the path. "Coming?"

She looked away as if she'd lost an argument, "I'm going back."

It struck me that I was no longer in love with her. I watched her saunter back along the path to her sister and her mother and Wilf's boat. Her hips were swaying quite noticeably, which I didn't mind watching at all. I think she knew I was still standing there.

The Tay Canal was as flat and brown as ever, and too murky to see much below the surface. Once we were through the upper lock, Wilf let his throttle out full blast and their boat soon edged away from ours, purring away at the rate of knots. We pottered along keeping steady at eight miles an hour. I wouldn't sneer at a faster engine, but this was nice. Ahead of us the water path wound its way among beds of cattails, taking a zig here and a zag there. Here and there, shoreline trees hung lazily over the water and, from their branches, crows haw-hawed at our slow progress. Auntie Lizzie leaned over my shoulder, pointing up at the sky. "It's going to be a long winter, I'll wager," she said.

We all looked up to where she was pointing. Canada geese getting an early start south formed an off-kilter, long-legged vee. And then we heard them beating the air with their wings and hollering questions at one another. At least that's what it sounded like, the way their voices went up in repetitious little question marks. "Where? Where? Where?" they gabbled. Ernie says I have an overdeveloped imagination, and he could be right. We watched some stragglers catch up to the short leg of the vee and no sooner had they joined it, than the whole thing wobbled out of shape, then reformed into a tidier vee, never changing direction. They went over us, altering, mending their formation, curious about their destination, but always moving forward, taking the right direction by instinct. We watched as they continued south until we lost sight of them.

THE END